ANOTHER NIGHT

At just before two a.m., newlywed Elizabeth Arnaud gasped as she heard the strident, urgent voice of a woman in the room. "Help! Help me!" Elizabeth struggled to awake. "He's going to kill me!" the words came.

Elizabeth put a hand to her mouth as she saw a female apparition calling from the corner of their compartment in a low, suppressed scream. Elizabeth cried out. Her husband, Tony, jolted awake now, reached for his new wife, saying, "*Mon Dieu!* Darling—what is it?"

"She was there—the Duchess, just like in your book—her spirit or ghost—blood all over her—oh, God!"

"No one is there, *chérie.*"

"Call the conductor, Tony! Bring him here—please!"

Arnaud hurriedly pulled on his clothes. "My poor bride . . . I'm sorry. . . . I'll find him. . . . I'll be right back."

Still dazed, Elizabeth shook her head and looked about the room. Her mind told her it couldn't be true. But all her senses said what she saw was real. She spoke in a hollow voice to herself, to their empty room, "She's still haunting the Orient Express."

THE CASE OF COMPARTMENT 7

A JOHN DARNELL MYSTERY

Sam McCarver

A SIGNET BOOK

SIGNET
Published by New American Library, a division of
Penguin Putnam Inc., 375 Hudson Street,
New York, New York 10014, U.S.A.
Penguin Books Ltd, 27 Wrights Lane,
London W8 5TZ, England
Penguin Books Australia Ltd,
Ringwood, Victoria, Australia
Penguin Books Canada Ltd, 10 Alcorn Avenue,
Toronto, Ontario, Canada M4V 3B2
Penguin Books (N.Z.) Ltd, 182–190 Wairau Road,
Auckland 10, New Zealand

Penguin Books Ltd, Registered Offices:
Harmondsworth, Middlesex, England

First published by Signet, an imprint of New American Library,
a division of Penguin Putnam Inc.

First Printing, February 2000
10 9 8 7 6 5 4 3 2 1

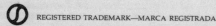

REGISTERED TRADEMARK—MARCA REGISTRADA

Printed in the United States of America

PUBLISHER'S NOTE
This is a work of fiction. Names, characters, places, and incidents either
are the product of the author's imagination or are used fictitiously,
and any resemblance to actual persons, living or dead, business estab-
lishments, events, or locales is entirely coincidental.

For Grace, Rose, Tyler,
and Trevor

ACKNOWLEDGMENTS

Almost seventy years ago, in 1934, Agatha Christie presented an enduring gift to the world in the form of her classic mystery novel *Murder on the Orient Express*—originally called *Murder on the Calais Coach* in America. Two years earlier Graham Greene's *Orient Express*, entitled *Stamboul Train* in England, had been published. Any author writing about the legendary train owes a literary debt to these great writers—and I definitely do.

Real-life persons are included in the story told in this book. However, except for their involvement in historically documented events, their participation in this story line derives from my imagination, since this book is a work of fiction. I thank Joseph Pittman, Senior Editor at New American Library, for his enthusiasm, perceptive editorial comments, and support. I value highly also NAL's eagle-eyed copy-editing staff for their thorough reviews, and the cover design staff for their sparkling creativity. For his ideas and encouragement, I thank also my literary agent, Donald Maass.

Prologue

The bloody apparition of a young woman seemed to hover in the air. It floated just above the floor of compartment seven of the Orient Express, in a dark corner across from the bed in which a gray-haired woman lay in fitful sleep.

Now the apparition spoke, or, more accurately, exuded the breath in her lungs in a low supplication, a suppressed scream. "Help. Help me." The words became louder. "Help! He's going to kill me!"

The woman sat upright in the bed, brushed her thinning hair back, and stared, wide-eyed, at the corner of her room. She blinked and rubbed her eyes at the vision of the young woman dressed in a gossamer nightgown and peignoir, drenched in blood. The apparition clutched her neck with one hand and pressed the other to her chest. Her neck dripped blood from a fresh wound, sliced cleanly, as if by a very sharp knife.

The wound seemed to have missed the jugular, yet had released a flood of blood down onto the woman's chest. Her nightgown and peignoir were soaked with blood, revealing the outline of her shapely breasts.

The elderly woman screamed, shrank back in her bed, and covered her eyes. As the sounds ceased reverberating in her ears and brain, she opened her eyes cautiously and peered at the dark corner of the room. She saw nothing there. The apparition had vanished.

Chapter One

April 15, 1914, 6:00 P.M.

John and Penny Darnell left their cab at the Gare de Lyon train station in Paris and hurried forward toward the massive building. Porters followed with their bags. A drizzle of fine rain greeted them, and the streets were dark and wet on this cool spring night.

"Oh, John, this is so exciting!" Penny looked up at the ancient brick train station that confronted them, the huge archways and the clock tower staring down upon them. "The Orient Express! I can't believe it."

"Remember, I'm here to work. This is a case."

"But it's our honeymoon at last! Two years since we've been married and you've just gone from one case to another. We need this time together. And this is the kind of case you should always have—a luxury room, travel, gourmet food. Ummm! I can't wait to see our compartment."

As they entered the building, Darnell directed the porters to follow them to the train with their baggage. He took his wife's arm. "All right, let's see that fabulous compartment where we'll spend six days together."

"Six whole days!"

Darnell surveyed the train with eager eyes as they approached it for their second trip together. He'd never forget their first trip two years earlier, meeting on the ill-fated voyage of the *Titanic*. Barely surviving that tragedy, Darnell brought a killer on board to justice, and unraveled the mystery jinx of cabin 13, which White Star's Chairman hired him to solve.

Now he faced a similar challenge, but the nature of the Orient Express trip seemed to offer no danger to Penny, or—despite her pleadings in London for the honeymoon—she wouldn't be here. Phantoms. He frowned, thinking of their harrowing trip on the *Titanic*. That trip made this case look easy.

Ahead, Darnell saw M. Pierre Bayard, General Manager of the Orient Express, standing by the side of the train, issuing orders, greeting passengers effusively as they boarded the train, looking about nervously and biting his nails. Darnell could see this last hour was critical for Bayard's preparation of his train for departure.

In his letter to Darnell, Bayard had explained that the Express left Paris promptly at seven p.m., taking passengers to their destinations, the mysterious cities in the East—Budapest, Bucharest, and, by ship, from Constanta to Constantinople. This night, Wednesday, was exactly one week after the teacher had been terrified by the apparition.

Darnell came up to the Manager. "M'sieur Bayard? John Darnell." He shook Bayard's hand. "And this is my wife, Penny."

Bayard offered her a light bow. "Madame, so pleased to have you on my train. I know you will enjoy." He turned to Darnell. "We must talk, Professor."

Darnell nodded, turning to his wife. "Penny, a conductor will show you to our compartment, and I'll follow along soon."

"Wonderful. I'll unpack and freshen up."

Darnell watched as she followed the conductor down the track to their compartment. At the door, she turned and waved at him, and he held his hand up in response.

He turned to the train manager. "You speak excellent English, M'sieur Bayard."

"Call me Pierre, Professor. I studied English in London. We'll meet with my Chief of Security—he's waiting for us in that office."

He gestured toward a station house, a glassed-in office a dozen feet square positioned in the corridor between the tracks, and walked toward it with Darnell.

Darnell eyed the manager. "Have there been any other sightings of this phantom, since you wrote?"

Bayard shook his head. "No. *Le bon Dieu*—he has taken sympathy on me."

Inside the office, Bayard nodded at its occupant. "Andre Vachel, Chief of Security, Professor John Darnell."

The two shook hands. Darnell took in Vachel's appearance in a glance—a fully uniformed, rotund man with a brush mustache, and wearing a leather-holstered gun strapped to his belt.

Vachel said, "They call me 'little bull.' That's what my name means." He showed his back gold teeth.

Bayard raised his eyebrows. "Vachel means 'little cow.' "

Vachel smiled. "That's for the women."

The three men sat in straight-backed chairs around the small table. Darnell said, "Tell me more about this sighting. Your letter said the woman called it an apparition."

"Yes, an apparition . . . but a letter cannot convey how she felt. She was hysterical."

"And, once more, she saw, exactly . . . ?"

Bayard grimaced. "A gruesome blood-drenched apparition—or phantom, as you wish—in her compartment, as I described it in the letter. I calmed her down by giving her free passage, if she would tell no one of her experience, and she agreed."

"You said in your letter, the elderly woman—a teacher I believe—was not harmed."

"No one—nothing at all—touched her."

"Then what is your main concern?"

"The Chairman of my Board of Directors. He let me know I must resolve this matter quickly, that we can't allow damage to the reputation of the Orient Express. We service European royalty, *nouveau de riche* tourists, and governmental couriers. 'Our coffers need European gold'—my Chairman's words. I'd heard of your reputation as an investigator of paranormal events and that you could explain this—and stop it from recurring."

"I suspect there's something substantial behind the event. These experiences don't just happen in a vacuum. If the background can be studied, almost always a rational explanation can be found. But you have to tell me everything."

Bayard glanced about the room and out the glass windows, as if afraid of being overheard. "We have tried to keep it secret."

"The time for secrets is over."

Bayard touched his brow with a handkerchief. "It happened many years ago—in 1886. The only employee left on the line who worked on the Orient Express at that time is Albert, the Chief Conductor on this train. He told me about it. There were no files, or, if there were, they were destroyed."

"Go on."

Bayard took a deep breath. "The great armaments baron Sir Basil Zaharoff occupied the compartment the teacher was in—number seven. At about two a.m., the first night out, he heard screaming and footsteps running in the corridor. He opened the door and saw a young, dark-haired woman running toward him from the other end, heading straight toward his open door. She was clutching her neck, which had been slashed, and was bleeding profusely down onto her chest. She wore nothing but a nightgown and loose peignoir."

"Exactly as the teacher described it."

"She reached Zaharoff's compartment door, saying, 'Help me, help me, he's going to kill me!' and Zaharoff caught her as she was falling to the floor. He lifted her and carried her to the bed."

"Who was going to kill her?"

"Her husband, the Duke. She was the Duchess Maria. They were on their honeymoon."

"Incredible."

"Zaharoff took care of her wounds. She stayed in his compartment that night, and never returned to her husband, who, it seems, had been taken by a fit of madness."

"Indeed."

"The husband was sent away for medical attention. The Duchess Maria was taken in by another royal family. It's rumored that Zaharoff and the Duchess still have liaisons in Paris, although they both remain married to others."

"The 1886 slashing was covered up—buried in your archives?"

"The story might turn away passengers. You understand."

"But it's back—and you put passengers in that compartment this trip?"

"It was too late to make a change. First class is full."

Darnell said, "Do you think there could be a hoax involved?"

Bayard shook his head. "The woman last week was a French history teacher on sabbatical from the Sorbonne in Paris. She seemed reliable. I never thought . . ."

"I understand." Darnell sat back and drummed his fingers on the table. "I'll need some information on the passengers."

Bayard nodded. "I've attended to that." He took two sheets of paper from his pocket. "Here's the complete passenger list, with some information on each, and staff. Your dinner companions for tonight are marked, also."

"Good. Well, I'll observe the passengers, one by one. My wife and I will dine with as many as we can, rotating from one to the other tables at breakfast, lunch, dinner. Penny will naturally draw out the women in conversation. Knowing something about all of them could be important, if anything happens on this trip."

"Do you have any ideas yet?"

"The world of spiritualism and psychic phenomena is filled with charlatans, Pierre, who prey on others they feel will readily accept the bizarre as reality. There are those who use a hoax for fame—in England, that's very common. I seek out both kinds. Often the so-called psychic events can be explained through understanding the people." He paused. "Of course, I'll want to inspect compartment seven, and talk with Albert."

Vachel spoke up with a growl, shaking his head.

"Only police methods can succeed. When I worked for the *Surete*—"

Bayard interrupted him. "Andre, *s'il vous plait!*" To Darnell, he said, "He would go on for hours about the *Surete*."

Bayard glanced at his watch. "Six-thirty. Let's prepare to board."

Darnell shook Vachel's hand again. "I appreciate your having men along the way. Let's hope I won't have to use their services."

Vachel gave him a stern look. "Be cautious, *mon ami*. In these times, the Orient Express is called the secret agent line, for good reason. Such agents guard their secrets with their lives."

The Security Chief watched from his office window as the two men worked their way back through the burgeoning crowd to the train. Vachel sat at his desk and removed a bottle of red wine he had quickly dropped into a drawer when the two entered. He refilled his glass and took a large swallow.

Darnell and Bayard walked back to the first-class and dining-car entrances of the train. As they reached that area, Darnell observed a frantic bustle of activities, including particularly the commotion of loading provisions. A tall man with a paunch and waxed mustachios supervised the loading. He wore a white apron and chef's hat, and bustled back and forth, giving orders to the men handling crates and baskets.

"That's Chef Voisseron," Bayard said. "Grand master of the kitchen. He's been chef for the Orient Express fifteen years now. He prides himself on his food and wines."

Darnell watched as provisions arrived. Voisseron removed crate lids and checked their contents. *"Mon Dieu!"* he shouted to a vendor. "These are oranges?

Tomatoes? Take these back to your truck and bring better ones." He glanced at the label of a bottle of red wine. "Cheap! Replace this with a good burgundy."

Darnell winked at Bayard as he saw how the chef presided, with great flourish and spectacle, over the loading of meats and vegetables, wines and liqueurs, champagne, cheeses and breads, caviar, fish, hens, fruits, boxes of cigars and chunks of ice.

"Everything looks delicious," Darnell said. "The Chef takes his work seriously."

"Wait until dinner. The chef surpasses himself the first night. You and your wife will enjoy his *haute cuisine.*"

Darnell checked the time. "I must board and find Penny."

"The conductor will escort you." Bayard snapped his fingers and a trim, blue-uniformed man hurried over to them.

"Louis, take Professor Darnell to compartment eight."

The conductor bowed and spoke in accented English, "This way, m'sieur."

"The dinner call is at eight," Bayard said.

Darnell followed the conductor. He looked forward to enjoying their luxurious compartment with Penny before dinner. A honeymoon at last. And a phantom, for good measure.

At ten minutes before seven p.m., Pierre Bayard looked anxiously up and down the length of the train, watching for two special passengers. Already he had made sure, personally, of the arrival of most of his guests, greeting them by name and providing them escorts to their compartments. Also, earlier, he had assured himself that Prince Carol II, the heir apparent of the Rumanian monarchy, was well settled into his private salon car.

But the two British couriers were late, and Bayard remembered cautions of the Board Chairman, the morning before, to take special care with them—Major Alexander Coulton and his assistant, Donald Brand. Bayard frowned as he found himself biting his fingernails, a habit he thought he had overcome.

Albert, the head conductor, pulled a gold watch from his pocket and clicked open the case. "*En voiture*," he called out in his strident voice. "All aboard."

Bayard cringed and checked his own watch: six fifty-five. The couriers might miss the train, or delay it.

Then he saw them, walking rapidly toward him from the station rotunda, followed by two porters carrying two suitcases each. The older man, obviously the Major, clutched his briefcase under his arm so tightly Bayard felt it would take much physical violence to wrench it away from him. They arrived at his side, breathless.

"Made it," the Major said, and blotted his forehead with a linen handkerchief. "We knew you wouldn't leave without us," he said, his eyes twinkling, and shook hands with Bayard.

"Never. But we must board, now." Bayard snapped his fingers, and a conductor ran over to them.

"Please take Major Coulton and Mr. Brand to compartment five."

The conductor, the two couriers, and the porters boarded. The head conductor again called "All aboard" in English and French, and Mr. Pierre Bayard stepped up into the train, sighing with relief. He started down the corridors in his customary long tour of the train, from the engine back to the caboose.

He prided himself on his knowledge of the details of the train and its passengers, knowing everything was in good shape, that nothing looked out of place. On this trip, that was more important to him than ever.

Chef Voisseron gazed up at the heavens with a smile, murmuring, *"Le bon Dieu,"* as his last provisions were loaded.

Voisseron stepped into the dining car and observed his senior chef, two junior chefs, and kitchen handymen at work. He spoke to the new senior chef, Paul Cobert, who had replaced his longtime senior man who had taken a position at the Ritz Hotel in New York. He hoped Cobert would be up to the grueling task of a six-day round trip, working in confined quarters to make over two dozen very particular passengers happy with their food and drink.

Every inch of space was taken up by stoves and other cooking facilities, storage of foodstuffs and beverages, and the huge iceboxes that occupied the front end of the car. The chef inspected the final crates of food.

He called his men around him to review the dinner plans and the status of dishes prepared or in process. The men were of a variety of different nationalities, but all understood both French and English. He spoke to them in a mixture of the two languages.

"Your attention please. Tonight's menu. Hors d'oeuvres—caviar and champagne. Consommé. Tomato aspic. *Poissons*—tonight the sea bass. *Viandes*— *rosbif, escalope de veau,* and *poulet.* And the wines." He asked Cobert, "Are you set?"

The other nodded. *"Oui.* By eight-fifteen, when the first morsels are to be served, everything will be in readiness."

"*Bon*. We will discuss the desserts later. To work, now."

Voisseron pulled a bottle of red wine from a crate, removed the cork, sniffed the bouquet and filled a wineglass. He swirled the liquid in the glass, sniffed it and took a long sip. "Ah," he breathed, and sat back on his chef's stool.

As he did the first night of every trip, he said, "It will be a long night." Sampling the wine was a pleasant duty. As resident sommelier, he would taste wine at each table in a small tin cup he would wear around his neck. He smiled at the thought.

Chapter Two

"To our honeymoon," John Darnell said, clinking his glass with Penny's. "Nice of Bayard to provide the champagne."

"It'll help you relax. You're too tense tonight."

"It's the case . . . but it's also our first time away together, and I want us to enjoy it." Darnell gazed at his wife with mixed feelings, with growing qualms at bringing her along on a trip that might involve danger. After all, a bloody ghost had been reported.

"We will, John."

Darnell shook off his dark thoughts. "Then let's drink to it."

They touched glasses again, and sipped their drinks.

"The cupboards have silk sheets and eiderdown counterpanes in them for the beds, John. Like sleeping in a palace."

He smiled. "All the comforts we'd like to have at home." He glanced at his watch. "Another hour is the dinner call. Eight o'clock."

"Who will we dine with tonight, do you know?"

"No matter. My eyes will be on you."

"As a detective, you'll examine everyone. But John . . . ?"

"All right. Bayard said our dinner arrangement for tonight was on a list of passengers he gave me. Each night will be different."

"Where's the list?"

Darnell pulled from his pocket the sheets Bayard had given him. "Here it is . . . Let's see . . . there are eight compartments in the first-class sleeper. German General Klaus Eberhardt in number one. Bayard's note says he's from headquarters in Berlin. Next to him in number two, a Dutch woman, Margaretha Geertruuda Zelle."

"One and two. These compartments have connecting doors. I wonder . . ."

"German and Dutch? Maybe. The occupant of the third is Anna Held, noted as being a rather famous musical comedy singer from the New York stage. In number four, there's a wine merchant—Anton Donnelli."

"I hope he brought a good supply with him." Penny smiled and made a motion of tipping a glass back.

"Compartment five—Major Alexander Coulton and a Donald Brand, British couriers from London."

"Spies!"

"Hardly. But as close to spies, I suppose, as we'll see on this trip. Then, number six, a nurse, Agatha Miller. And number seven, Tony Arnaud and Elizabeth Hopkins Arnaud, two newlyweds on their honeymoon."

"I'm feeling like a newlywed, John. Are you?"

"Yes, dear—but one with a job to do." Darnell flipped to the second sheet. "In the second coach—second class, I assume—the first compartment is occupied by two Turks. I won't try to pronounce their last names—the first names are Gaspar and Nasim. And in the second compartment, two Greeks, Argus and Demetrius. Now here's an interesting one—Madame Yolanda Morgana. Some kind of mystic, Bayard says . . . She's on our dinner table list."

"Hmm. Fascinating."

"We'll also have the two couriers with us for dinner tonight, and the nurse." He studied the list. "Then there's a young man, by himself. Something to do with airplane designing, it says here. Bryan Stark, from England."

He tucked the sheets back in his pocket. "Beyond that, there's a couple of unoccupied rooms in the second coach, then Bayard's room, and Chef Voisseron's, assistant chefs, engineers, conductors, and so on, near the back of that coach."

Penny moved to his side. "I like ours."

"Compartment eight is as private as could be, on one side of it anyway, being last in this coach."

"That Madame—do you know any more about her?"

Darnell laughed. "Maybe she tells fortunes. Want to know yours?"

"You're my fortune."

Darnell mused. "I'm looking for a phantom, a ghost, an apparition, whatever it is. It'll be interesting to see if a psychic claims to sense anything unworldly on this train."

Penny wrinkled her brow. "But a ghost, if there is one, is from the past. Doesn't a psychic predict the future?"

"Past, present, future. They're all connected."

At that moment, they felt a jar as the train jerked from its standing start, chugging and inching forward with the thrust of the powerful engine. The wheels' rumble reached their ears.

Penny grabbed his arm. "We're moving!"

Darnell could imagine the steam belching from the engine's boiler through the cylinders, driving the piston rods, turning the wheels—slowly at first, then steadily faster as the engineer, with a practiced, measured hand, released power from the great boiler. The Orient Express had begun yet another journey, and the sound of the iron wheels on the track reverberated through the car. The Express would take its passengers through a panorama of lands many had heard of only in story and legend.

Knowing his own purposes for this case, Darnell wondered if this trip would take on a different character from the usual vacationers' luxurious escape from the humdrum.

Looking out of the window, Penny broke into his thoughts with a more personal analysis as the train rolled out of the station. "John! Our honeymoon is beginning!"

General Klaus Eberhardt raised his glass to his companion, a sultry, dark-haired, shapely woman whose gaze bore disturbingly into his eyes. "To us, my dear," the General said.

She smiled, her gaze not leaving his, and lifted a glass to her bright red lips. *"A votre sante."*

The woman gestured with her glass toward the open connecting door between their compartments. "Very thoughtful, Klaus."

"The ticket master was very accommodating. An extra two hundred marks assured us of compartments one and two."

"And he'll keep my identity secret?"

"Frankly, Mata, I don't think he suspects a thing. I doubt that he's seen you dance at the Folies Bergère."

"No one must know. If they suspected Mata Hari was aboard—well, I'd get no privacy. Call me by my real name, Margaretha or just Margaret. And remember the last name, Zelle."

"You want privacy even in bed?" The General smiled.

"Shame," the woman teased. "You embarrass me."

"Ha! Embarrass Mata Hari? A King would melt in the heat of your charm. Mata Hari—the sun." He put down his glass and took her in his arms. "Let me taste your lips, sweet with wine."

Mata Hari tipped her glass back and emptied it. She set it down and pressed her moist lips on the General's. "We have an hour until dinner," she murmured.

In compartment three, a coquettish, if aging, black-haired woman sat holding her orange Pomeranian dog. She stared out of the window as the train chugged away from the station.

An observer would say Anna Held's blue eyes were filled with an ineffable sadness as she stroked the soft hair of the small dog. "It's just you and me, now, Henri. I don't know where Flo is. Perhaps with his young actress—that floozy!" She petted her dog. "Oh, excuse me, Henri, I shouldn't use such language." Tears welled in her eyes. "But when I think of him, the Great Ziegfeld, throwing me over for a younger woman—oh, I can't stand it."

She brushed the tears away. "Maybe Philippe will be my cure, my little *poupée*. Did I tell you he boards at Vienna? Yes, Henri, and you will like him. He, too, will call you a doll."

She stroked the dog's back. "My doll. Here I am, forty-one, a useless ex-actress. Except for my jewelry, you're all I have left from all those years in America." Tears flowed again. "Ziegfeld and his follies. He was my folly." Mesmerized by memories, Anna Held stared at dark streets and distant buildings as the train followed the curving tracks out of

Paris, working its way slowly on the first leg of its long, tortuous journey.

Arturo Donatello lay on his bed in compartment four, smoking a cheroot as he studied a passenger list. Paying the stationmaster a hundred francs to get the list was well worth it.

This was a new way of identifying his potential victims—or should he call them his contributors? Which passengers, he wondered, would be traveling with their jewels, able to make some involuntary donations to his increasingly extravagant lifestyle?

He looked at his name on the list—Anton Donnelli. A good alias, similar but not too close to Arturo Donatello. Same initials on his cases. And his wine merchant profession cover story was good. He was pleased with his plans.

His thoughts were interrupted by the sound of sobbing from the next compartment. A woman's mature voice, sobbing heavily. A weariness was evident in her voice—a resignation, even a note of desperation. He glanced at his list—Anna Held. The name seemed familiar, but he could not place it. The crying ceased, and he listened, but heard no movement in the cabin. Then he heard a small yap. It was a small dog. And he remembered her.

He had watched her board the train. She was an attractive woman, about his age, with a very small waist and shapely body. She carried a small, orange-colored dog. An actress, perhaps. Such a woman should have jewels, he decided, returning to his main interest. And yet—something about her sobbing, the intensity of it, reached a sensitivity level in him he did not know he possessed. He would speak with her at dinner.

He smoothed his mustache thoughtfully and resumed his study of the others on the passenger list. A General and his apparent consort, couriers, a nurse, two newlyweds, a professor and his wife. He tossed the list down. Could this be a dry run? Then he recalled the special salon car with a European Prince.

Now, that, Donatello said to himself, offered good possibilities. And he loved the danger that it would imply to steal from a Prince. Perhaps this trip would not be wasted after all. And the woman next door— the sobbing woman. She was a sad woman, who might need comforting. Yes, he would introduce Anton Donnelli to her this very night.

Major Alexander Coulton directed Donald Brand as the young man stored their clothing in the small drawers and put their toilet articles above the marble sink in compartment five. At the window, Coulton allowed the scenery to flash by without comment. The train sped through Paris suburbs now, displaying greenery in place of the ramshackle buildings that lined the tracks in the city. He saw it without thinking of it. His mind focused on his mission: Transmit the documents as instructed. As a retired Boer War commander, he was used to taking and issuing orders, the army way—following orders, questioning nothing.

The Major watched Brand as he unpacked their things. He reflected that, for a courier, the young man was remarkably naive and uncurious. When he was Brand's age—well, that was another era, perhaps, an age of adventure. Brand seemed more interested in the people he met on their trips, rather than their mission.

He knew that today, the opportunity for personal adventure was limited by strict instructions from the

War Office. Yet he understood duty, and duty was sometimes vital, even if boring. But Brand . . .

"Shall I put your case up, Major?" Brand looked at his superior in what the Major regarded as a rare display of interest.

"No, of course not," Coulton responded with a haughtiness he did not realize he had in his voice. "I keep this with me at all times. Even at meals. I sleep with it. Clear enough? It's with me at all times."

"Yes, sir." But he shocked the Major by asking with a lilt in his voice, "Even when you bathe, sir?"

The young nurse in the next compartment liked traveling, particularly traveling alone, as she was on this trip. It gave her more time to write.

She loved making notes about people, observing them and thinking of them as characters for her stories. As yet, her writing had achieved only limited success, but she had in mind a grand plan. She would write adventure, suspense, or mystery novels, set in exotic lands and cities she could travel to for research, such as she would do on this trip. Places like Budapest and Bucharest. Places she could work into her plots and put in her books.

Agatha Miller shivered excitedly, thinking of adventures that could await her on this trip. Imagine, the Orient Express, and she was on it at the tender age of only twenty-three! In her wildest dreams she had imagined taking such a trip only as an old dowager.

She thought of her benefactor, E. W. Hornung. He had admired her writing talent enough to agree to pay for her trip. She wondered whether the jealousy he showed toward his brother-in-law, Arthur Conan Doyle, had influenced him to encourage new writers.

Did he want to offer more competition to Doyle's works through new novelists, producing works similar to the Raffles mysteries that Hornung wrote himself? Well, if he had a bad case of literary envy, it was a boon to her writing. She needed it, and accepted it.

A single light burned above the table in the second-class compartment. Spread out on the table were detailed plans and drawings, pencils, and a magnifying glass for the small details. Bryan Stark adjusted his gold-rimmed spectacles and studied the familiar plans with a gleam in his eye. The Farnborough, single-seat, B.S.I.! What government would not pay a small fortune to get a fleet of them with the rampant rumors of war? Planes would make the difference between victory and defeat. He was sure of it.

With his employer and mentor Geoffrey de Havilland on a holiday, Stark knew he could get to Budapest and back within the week, and no one would miss the plans, which could be copied, and none be the wiser. He rubbed his hands together in contemplation of his visit to the Hungarian War Office. Stark felt he had never received his due from de Havilland, who, still in his early thirties, was admittedly an aeronautical genius. Typical of the genius type, he felt, de Havilland was not one to lavish praise on others where it was due. Others would appreciate him more.

Stark frowned as he thought of the injustice. After all, who drew these plans out in detail? Who did the research and painstaking preparatory work? Now he would get the praise he deserved, and make a fortune.

Within a few years, Bryan Stark dreamed, I can have my own company, do my own designs, and I'll still be under thirty. Aloud, he said to the walls of his compartment, "Then everyone will know I was the real genius."

In first-class compartment seven, Elizabeth Hopkins Arnaud pressed her lips upon those of her husband, Tony. "Darling, I'm so happy."

"My *chérie*! My wife. Is this not *màgnifique*?"

"Yes. I can't believe it. Our honeymoon. Two weeks." She laughed. "Father will have a fit."

Tony's brow creased. "I hope your papa doesn't miss the money you took from their hotel room. What do you think he will do?"

Elizabeth laughed merrily, with the gaiety of a new bride. "He'll never miss it. I left a note. And if he does, what's a few hundred pounds. He must have thousands. Millions! I don't know."

Tony Arnaud's eyes narrowed. He stared ahead, but looked inward. "He will think . . . it is for the money, I marry you."

"Nonsense."

"He will say I am, what you call, the fortune-hunter."

She shook her head. "Someday you'll sell your paintings, and we'll be rich, too. Without his money. And mother dotes on you."

"Ye-es. She liked my portrait of her." He smiled. "Of course, I usually paint nudes."

Elizabeth laughed. "Mother as a nude. How rich! I'd love to see a painting of her that way."

"It's your father I worry about," Tony said. "He warned us we should not, how do you say . . . ?"

"Elope. But we couldn't wait, could we? He'll understand. I can make Father understand things, you know."

She looked about their compartment, at their suitcases. "We can put our things away after dinner. Come, hold me again. My husband . . ."

Tony Arnaud stopped her words with his lips. He clicked the lights off with the switch. Their compartment was lit now only by transient lights that flashed into the room as the train rumbled past villages and train stations. And the ancient sounds of young lovers syncopated with the hypnotic rhythm of the wheels of the Orient Express in the dark of compartment seven.

Chapter Three

The eight o'clock call to dinner brought with it an air of excitement. As Darnell walked forward with Penny, he saw that the sleeping-car first-class passengers had changed into their best clothing, the men into evening clothes, the women into flowing gowns.

They entered the dining car and heard a string quartet playing in an alcove just inside the door.

"John," Penny said, "they're playing Chopin. Isn't that wonderful?" She smiled at the violinist, and received a bright smile and a nod of the head in reply.

After the waiter seated them, Darnell said, "There's a palpable feeling of excitement here. Almost like a ship embarking. It's so much like our first night out on the *Titanic*, Penny." His words brought memories flashing back through his mind of their first night on the ship—and that terrifying last night.

But she was inspecting the room. "Look at the paintings, John. That's a Delacroix. The others are exquisite, too."

Darnell heard raucous laughter coming from the end of the car and turned his head to observe a table where four men sat. "The Turks and Greeks seem happy enough."

"Who are they?"

"The conductor told me they all just use their first names—Gaspar, Nasim, Demetrius, and Argus—that he couldn't pronounce their last names. Said they've traveled this route before, always together. They're staying in the second car."

"Here come some of our dinner companions. Two women," Penny whispered. "Look at the older woman's dress, the sequins, those great strands of pearls."

"Befitting a psychic," he said. "That has to be the Madame." Privately he thought, It's a bit overdone, but she's a performer of sorts. He realized he had begun his evaluation of the passengers.

Darnell stood as the two women approached. "Madame Yolanda Morgana, I believe, and you must be Miss Agatha Miller. I'm Professor John Darnell, and this is my wife, Penny."

The women shook hands, exchanged pleasantries, complimented one another on their gowns.

As they talked, the waiter brought two men forward to their table, and the British couriers were introduced all around the table. Major Coulton placed his sturdy brown leather four-inch-thick briefcase under his chair, next to the window.

Agatha Miller spoke to Penny. "Isn't this table service elegant? I've never seen such silver and real china. Napkins folded to look like birds. And the walls— inlaid mahogany, carved woods, and the arched ceilings. I can't wait to write it down."

"If you're taking notes, the chandelier is magnificent, too," Penny responded. "Imagine that on a train."

The room was filling up, and Darnell studied the passengers as waiters seated them. Manager Pierre Bayard stopped and spoke briefly with Darnell, then took his own seat at a table with a uniformed German General and a dark-haired petite woman who had the smoothest complexion Darnell had ever seen.

Two young people looking newly married came in smiling, peering at the decor with wide eyes. A sad-eyed but beautiful woman "of a certain age" sat alone at a small table. In a few minutes, she was joined by a suave-looking mustachioed man with a Mediterranean look. He stopped at the table, bowed, introduced himself, and when she nodded and smiled, took a seat opposite her.

Penny whispered to Darnell, "That woman you seem to be studying is attractive, isn't she? With that hourglass figure?"

He smiled. "Can't say I noticed."

The evening was a gala event. The music created a festive mood. The waiters, themselves in evening clothes, bustled back and forth serving appetizers and champagne, while the Manager shuttled from table to table greeting passengers. The dining car was lightly occupied this night, at only half of its capacity, making for a more comfortable dining experience.

Major Coulton licked his lips when the waiters brought champagne, caviar, and toast points. "Food," he said. "And such food it is. To our trip," he said, holding out his fluted glass to the others. "May we all enjoy it."

They all touched glasses, and sipped their drinks.

"Courier work must be exciting," Agatha Miller remarked to the Major and his assistant, across from her. "I'd love to write about spies and foreign agents."

The major shook his head. "Oh, we're not spies, I can assure you. Nothing like that. Just messengers." The Major laughed easily. "Right, Donald?"

Donald Brand nodded. But his gaze was fixed on the young woman. "You write novels, Miss Miller?"

"Not yet." She shook her tight curls from side to side. "Just short pieces. But I hope to do that. Maybe you two can give me some ideas."

Brand's eyes brightened. "Gladly."

Madame Morgana's gaze moved from one to the other of her fellow diners, as if assessing their psychic or commercial possibilities, settling at last on Darnell's countenance, on her right. "You have a special mission," she murmured. "Something of importance."

Darnell laughed lightly. "I've heard of your skills in telling fortunes, Madame. Do you read minds, too?"

"No, no. But I sense a purpose behind you."

Penny spoke up. "We do have a purpose. It's our honeymoon, one we were unable to take for two years because of John's work." She paused. "But do tell us about your fortune-telling."

The Madame's eyes glistened and took on a far-away look. "I predict world events, for the most part. I do it in stanzas. I have been called the female Nostradamus."

"I never understood his mysterious language, or peculiar symbolism," Penny said.

Madame Morgana shook her head. "He disguised his work. He had to, or he might have been killed by those he offended."

"And your works?"

"My quatrains are more direct. I deal with the world of the near future, not hundreds of years from now. But, of course, I also do predictions for individuals who want help in their lives." She looked around the table.

Agatha Miller's eyes sparkled. "British spies and a psychic at my table. Wait 'till mother hears of this."

The Madame's face took on a sterner look. "I return to Bucharest from London after a year. I feel I must be in my homeland to be safe. I tell all of you this—I feel a sense of dread on this trip. I smell it. The vibrations are strong."

"Smells and vibrations," Penny said, smiling. "Maybe the smells are the garlic? The vibrations from the train wheels?"

The Madame sniffed. "Make fun if you will. Perhaps my feelings come from the passengers, the train itself, or the world out there we pass by. But I do feel this. And I sense danger."

The food service came, interrupting their conversations. Chef Voisseron opened wine bottles at each table with a flourish, tasting the wine from his small steel cup, exclaiming, in each case, his delight at the bouquet, the nose, the flavor. White wine with fish. Red, later, with the *viands*, he recommended. Let it breathe. After each taste he became more relaxed.

Waiters brought food then, beginning with the consommé. The menu outlined by Chef Voisseron earlier that day proceeded.

The chef moved from table to table, shaking hands, asking passengers whether they had special preferences for sauces.

He moved back and forth from the kitchen to the dining room to supervise dishes, to observe his passengers, to see to their comfort. The chef, as all could see, was in his glory.

After they had finished their main courses and the polite conversation interspersed with servings of their food, Agatha Miller again addressed Madame Morgana. "Can you give us any predictions tonight, Madame?"

The other nodded, put down her fork, and ceremoniously touched her lips with a napkin. She looked about as if to see whether she had the attention of all at the table. "I'll read you what I wrote this evening after I boarded the Express." She took a single sheet of paper from her handbag and unfolded it dramatically.

She paused, glanced around the table, and read:

> *"Inferno beckons us, the hot flame attracts,*
> *while armies of Europe plan their attacks*
> *on bastions of their neighbors' world.*
> *The flags of war will be soon unfurled."*

Darnell said, "That's very direct. Do you see war soon?"

She shook her head, her pearls jangling back and forth. "My visions have no exact timetable. I will say—not very long."

"Balderdash!" Major Coulton said. "We'll have treaties. We will forestall any war. Wiser heads will prevail."

Madame Morgana fixed the gaze of her impenetrable dark eyes on his. "I hope, Major, that you live to see that your words are more prophetic than mine. The war clouds are heavy, and the downpour will inevitably come."

Penny laughed. "You're mixing your metaphors, Madame. That downpour might put out the fires you've got in your quatrain."

Agatha Miller said, "I love it! Psychics, spies, intrigue!"

After dessert, Agatha Miller left the dining room, the newlyweds remarked they were going to their compartment, and the Turks and Greeks walked out, arm in arm, singing something raucous in a foreign tongue.

The other women strolled back to the ladies' salon

car. They relaxed in plush seats in the silk-draped room, enjoying tea and cream puffs. After whispered words to Madame Morgana, Anna Held left for her compartment saying she must feed her dog. Mata Hari, calling herself Margaret Zelle, spoke of Paris with Penny.

Darnell and Pierre Bayard adjourned to the leather seats of the men's lounge, where they smoked and sipped Napoleon brandy. The bookcases there went untouched as a discussion ensued among Darnell, the British couriers, and General Eberhardt on war rumblings. When the talk became heated between the two Britishers and the German, the Major left. By 12:30 A.M. all had retired.

Afterward, in the privacy of their lush compartments in the first class car, lights out, passengers were soon rocked to sleep by the hypnotic rhythm and sounds of the train as they lay listening to the click-clacking of the wheels in the dark of night, and the occasional shrill sound of the steam whistle as the train passed through small villages along the way.

Bryan Stark lay on his bed staring at the ceiling, listening to the sounds of the train, thinking of the aircraft plans rolled up and secured in his suitcase. He had dined alone at a small table and avoided the men's smoking salon. The less conversation he indulged in, the less he would have to answer prying questions and expose his purposes. Yet the presence of the Rumanian Prince and the German General on the train was an unexpected development. Should he approach them with the aircraft plans? Their money was as good as any. He would have to find a way of doing that without causing a scene.

Nervous, although gaining more confidence with every mile he distanced himself from London, Stark tossed and turned in his bed and at length fell into a fitful sleep.

General Eberhardt and Mata Hari lay in the General's bed, his compartment illuminated only by the flickering of a candle she had lit and placed on the ledge of the window. His breathing was heavy. The dancer who had become a spy lay quietly next to him. Her thoughts swirled with plans. Sleep was not part of them.

Anna Held slept fitfully, tossing and turning. In the next compartment, Arturo Donatello listened to her occasional sleep sounds, thinking of their conversation together at dinner, and of her distress.

In compartment five, in his lower bunk, Major Coulton snored. His assistant, Brand, lay in the bunk above him, eyes open, staring at the ceiling, listening to the annoying snoring sounds coming from below, wondering why the government couldn't pay for each to have a compartment of his own.

In number six, after finishing her story notes for the night and tucking them away carefully into her portfolio, Agatha Miller climbed into her bed. "I know I'll dream of spies tonight," she told herself. Within minutes, she slumbered peacefully.

Comfortable and happy to have the luxury and privacy of their coach-end compartment, pleased and excited with the trip, John Darnell and Penny listened to the train's sounds as it trundled along the fields and distant hills and past villages in the night, and relished their time together. They fell asleep, lying quietly in each other's arms.

In compartment seven, Elizabeth and Tony Arnaud talked of their honeymoon plans and their future. "What's that little book you're carrying around?" Elizabeth asked.

He pulled a slim volume from his pocket and said,

"Some stories from the train's early days. I'll have to read it to you—it's in French."

"I love stories. Are they scary?"

Elizabeth sipped champagne as he read, and shivered deliciously at the stories.

After a while she touched his arm and said, "Put that book down and come to my arms."

They finished their champagne and reveled in their plush surroundings on this first night of marriage, which enhanced the excitement and wonder of their tender lovemaking. Afterward, the new young bridegroom and his bride lay entangled in each other's arms. She stirred in her sleep, making murmurs her bridegroom would have found endearing, had he been awake. Nine hours since their wedding, and they were in the deep, relaxed sleep of newlyweds.

At just before two a.m., Elizabeth gasped as she heard the strident, urgent voice of a woman in the room. "Help! Help me!" Elizabeth struggled to awake. "He's going to kill me!" the words came.

Elizabeth put a hand to her mouth and stared at the source of the words, and saw a female apparition calling out from the corner of their compartment in a low, suppressed scream. Elizabeth rubbed her eyes and cried out. Her husband, jolted awake now, reached out for his new wife. He took her in his arms and said, "*Mon Dieu!* Darling—what is it?"

His bride sat up, burst into tears, and pointed at the dark corner of the compartment. "She was there—the Duchess, just like in your book—her spirit or ghost—blood all over her—oh, God!"

Arnaud held her close. "Shuh, shuh, *bébé*. It's all right, now. I'm here."

"She's gone now—did you see her, Tony?" Elizabeth sobbed in his arms.

"No one is there, *chérie*."

"She was there, I know it. I felt I could reach out and touch her." She shuddered. "She had blood running down all over her nightgown—you know, her *chemise de nuit.*"

Arnaud frowned. "My poor bride . . . I'm sorry . . ."

Elizabeth stared again at the spot where the apparition had floated in the corner. She pulled the covers up about her neck and shuddered again, her good English sense slowly coming back. "Call the conductor, Tony. Tell him about this phantom—bring him here—please!"

Arnaud hurriedly pulled on shoes, pants, and a dressing gown. "I'll find him . . . I'll be right back."

Elizabeth Arnaud, still dazed, shook her head and looked about the room. Her mind told her it couldn't be true. But all her senses said what she saw was real. She spoke in a hollow voice to herself, to their empty room. "She's still haunting the Orient Express."

Chapter Four

Tony Arnaud ran down the corridor, found the conductor, and brought him back to compartment seven, where his wife huddled in the corner of the bed, blankets pulled up to her neck. When the conductor heard the brief outlines of the story of the apparition, he quickly excused himself, saying he must bring the Manager himself into this.

When he and Bayard returned to the compartment, they found Darnell dressed in trousers and his Chinese robe and standing at the door of number seven.

"I heard the screams through the wall of our compartment, and dressed as quickly as I could."

"Let's go in," Bayard said, and the three entered.

"Tell us what happened, from the beginning," Bayard said to Tony Arnaud.

"It was horrible," Elizabeth began, her voice quavering. "It was like a ghost. She was only wearing a nightgown and a peignoir over it. She had blood all over her, on her chest, dripping down from her neck, everywhere." Elizabeth shuddered. "Her neck had a fiery red gash in it, and it was bleeding down onto her chest."

"You weren't having a nightmare, madame?" Darnell studied her. "You're certain of that?" He looked about the room carefully as she answered, but saw nothing unusual.

"No," she said. "It was real. Too real. She spoke to me. 'Help,' she said, and again. Then, 'He's going to kill me.'"

Bayard looked at the husband. "You saw it, too?"

He put his arm around Elizabeth. "You doubt my wife? Her horrible screams woke me. They were real. I attended her. She felt something was in the room, and I believe her . . . but after I comforted her, we looked about again, and, whatever it was, it was gone."

Bayard sighed. "I'm very sorry, madame. This is unheard of, I assure you. Do you want to move to a different compartment? We have some vacant in the second car."

"No, no, not second class," Elizabeth said. She looked at her husband. "This is our honeymoon, Tony."

Tony scowled. "But this is not right. It is spoiling our trip. I have heard of such a thing happening before, on the *Orient Express*—a phantom, a ghost. Was there something last week? Was this it?"

Bayard cringed. A second phantom sighting within a week would infuriate his Board. His solution the first time might work again. He looked at Darnall, who nodded as if to say, proceed. "I have one thing to offer you," Bayard urged, "if you will not move to another space. We will give you free passage to your destination and return . . . refund your fares. But there would be one condition."

Tony Arnaud's eyes narrowed. "And that would be . . . ?"

"You must tell no one of this, neither on this train nor later. It must remain within this room, between us. Is that agreed?"

"You don't want to scare the passengers." Tony smiled. He looked at Elizabeth. "If my wife agrees, I agree."

Elizabeth nodded.

"But if it happens again . . ." Tony said.

Bayard nodded vigorously. "Then we do more. We hope the rest of the evening is uneventful. M'sieur Arnaud, come by my compartment tomorrow for your refund voucher."

Darnell said, "I'm right next door, Mr. Arnaud. If anything happens again tonight, or any night, pound on my door. I'll do everything I can to help."

In the corridor, the three stood talking. Bayard told his chief conductor, "Not a word of this, Albert."

The conductor nodded, but said, "Do you think . . . ?"

"We do not think, Albert. We go back to work. Is that clear?"

Albert nodded and walked down the corridor. When he was out of earshot, Bayard turned to Darnell. "Now we have our ghost again. What do we do, John? You're the expert."

Darnell mused. He touched the raised numeral on the door. "Seven is considered a lucky number, but in this case . . ." He considered the situation. "We wait and watch. We make sure they do not discuss it with the other passengers, as you asked. I know your interest is not disturbing other passengers. You may want to get an assurance from the Arnauds in writing at the end of the trip as to their silence."

"But the phantom?"

"No one was harmed. It's gone, for now. If she makes another appearance—in dreams or otherwise—we'll deal it then."

"In dreams? The woman said it was not a dream."

"But we can't rule it out. I know she protested it wasn't one, but a nightmare could seem very real to a very young, impressionable woman, intoxicated with champagne and excited by her first night of marriage."

"But in the same compartment, an old woman, a young woman? Twice? A week apart?"

Darnell nodded. "The double sighting factor may be a vital part of the mystery. Sightings of this nature tend to cluster. Some call it group self-hypnosis, others say merely a compounding of rumor. Whatever it is, I wouldn't be surprised if we hear more about our bloody Duchess before this trip is over."

Darnell had to tell Penny the story from beginning to end, describing the woman's experience with the sighting, before she would allow him to get any sleep. By four a.m. they were both asleep again, and heard nothing until the eight a.m. breakfast call. They dressed and joined the others in the dining car.

Elizabeth and Tony Arnaud were seated at their separate table for two. Darnell stopped momentarily as he and Penny passed by and asked Tony and Elizabeth softly, "Everything all right? Were you able to sleep?"

The two nodded, said they had managed, and offered tentative smiles of reassurance. But Darnell saw that Elizabeth's eyes were bloodshot.

At their appointed table, the Darnells were joined by Bayard, Agatha Miller and the junior courier, Donald Brand.

"And the Major?" Darnell asked. "He will be coming?"

Brand shook his head. "Still asleep. He told me he never breakfasts, and not to wake him. He'll have coffee later." He turned to the young nurse, his eyes taking in her fresh morning look, in a pink flowered dress. "How are you, Miss Miller?"

"Very well. Before I fell asleep I wrote some good notes of our conversation last night. I'm getting some ideas for a story, maybe on a boat or a train." Her gaze drifted toward the window and she watched the scenery as it seemed to speed by them. "Even this train, perhaps . . ."

"You spend a lot of your time writing," Brand said, "but I understand you're a nurse."

She laughed. "One must have an occupation—that is, one that produces income. Writing is, well, unpredictable at best."

As they talked, several other passengers drifted in, singly or in couples, and took seats. The Turks and Greeks arrived and ordered champagne noisily.

Darnell noticed that the two beauties of the trip— the dark-haired women who had sat at other tables the night before—were late in arriving. Minutes later the General arrived and took a seat with one of them, and the slick, mustachioed gentleman with an Italian look sat with the second. Madame Yolanda Morgana was nowhere to be seen.

The waiter brought coffee and menus. All ordered, and shortly they were busy with coffee, porridge, crisp toast, eggs, and bowls of local berries. Champagne was offered, but at their table only Brand accepted a single glass. Bayard was unusually silent and looked glum.

"I'd like to tour all the cars with you after breakfast," Darnell said to the Manager. That would give them time to talk, he thought, and compare notes.

Bayard nodded, but said nothing.

After their meal, Darnell escorted Penny to the ladies' salon, where she proposed to do some reading.

Penny found Madame Morgana there sipping tea and sat near her.

"Tea is all I ever have," the psychic said. The two began a conversation.

Darnell met Bayard again back in the dining room, prepared to take their tour. They sat at a table at the far end.

"They'll be clearing tables," Bayard said, "and putting on fresh cloths and silver for the next meal, beginning at the other end. Otherwise we have the room to ourselves."

"About last night . . ." Darnell began.

Donald Brand burst through the doorway of the coach at the other end. He looked about at the waiters with his eyes wild. Then he saw Bayard and Darnell and ran to their table. "Thank God you're here! Come quickly! I think the Major is dead."

Bayard spilled his coffee as he stood. "Dead? Are you sure?"

"I think so. Come with me, please. Hurry!"

Brand turned and ran back toward his compartment, Bayard and Darnell following at his heels. Reaching compartment five, Brand opened the door wide and said, "You can see him. Lifeless. I didn't touch him."

Bayard said, "Stand back, Brand. The Professor and I will examine him." They stepped inside. Brand followed, closed the door behind them, and leaned against it.

The Major lay fully dressed on his bed, eyes closed, as if asleep. But one arm dangled loosely at the side of the bed. Beneath his hand, a water tumbler lay on the carpet, tipped sideways, a bit of liquid remaining in it.

Darnell checked the Major's pulse, and shook his head. With a handkerchief, he picked up the glass and sniffed the liquid. "Poison," he said. "The almond odor."

"Is it suicide?" Bayard bit his fingernails nervously.

Darnell turned to Brand, who stared at the Major's body with glassy eyes. "What do you know of this?"

The young man shook his head. "Nothing. He just seemed to be sleeping when I left our room for breakfast. When I returned, I saw him—just as you find him now."

"Did he say anything last night, or give any indication he might . . . ?"

"Commit suicide? No. But senior couriers do carry a poison pill, I know that, just as government agents do. In case they could be forced to reveal their secrets. There's a pledge they take."

"No evidence of theft." Darnell glanced about the room.

"No." Brand looked under the Major's bed. "His case is here." He stepped over and picked it up. "It's still locked."

"And the key?"

"He kept it on a gold bracelet on his wrist at night. Shall I . . . ?"

Darnell nodded.

Brand slipped the Major's sleeve up an inch on the right wrist. "The key's here," he announced. "I'll take custody of it." He slipped off the bracelet and dropped it into his coat pocket. "I guess I'm in charge of the Major's briefcase now, at least until I can reach someone in authority." He ran a hand through his hair.

Bayard cleared his throat, as if testing whether he could speak at all. "We'll move his body to the caboose until we reach the next stop." He glanced at his watch. "That would be Ulm. We'll turn it over to the police there, and you may be able to reach your people." He slumped into a chair and rubbed his temples. "My head," he mumbled. "Last night. Now a suicide. What next?"

Darnell prowled about the small room, checked above the sink. An open bottle of scotch and a glass stood on the sink. "This other glass is wet, as if it's been rinsed."

"Someone else used it?"

His face grim, Darnell nodded. "Used it—probably with scotch—then cleaned it. The fact that the Major was dressed and was drinking, and this second glass—well, it seems to show he had a visitor this morning while we were at breakfast. And if he had a visitor, we must certainly suspect murder."

Chapter Five

After recruiting two conductors to move the body to the caboose, Bayard and Darnell stood there in the coolness of the unheated caboose talking of their next steps. "There's no doctor on the train," Bayard said. "We can't get an opinion on the poison aspect."

"But we have a nurse. Miss Miller," Darnell said. "We should see if she can be of any help."

"There's little she can do, not more than a junior in that field." Bayard hesitated. "All right. Follow me." He led the way to sleeping car number six and rapped on the door.

When Agatha Miller opened it, her eyes brightened and she smiled at them. "Well, hello." But as her eyes flicked from one to the other, her smile quickly faded. "What's happened?"

"May we step in for a moment?"

"Of course, M'sieur Bayard, Professor. Is something wrong?"

The Manager closed the door behind them. "I'll come straight to the point. You may have heard some commotion next door?"

"Ye-es. The door slamming. Footsteps."

"Major Coulton has died. And it is not *belle mort*." Agatha Miller frowned. "Dead?" The nurse in her came to the surface as she probed. "Not a natural death? So, that leaves an accident, suicide, or . . . murder."

Bayard spoke quickly. "It may have been suicide." He turned to Darnell. "The glass?"

Darnell produced the Major's glass from his coat pocket. "The Major didn't come to breakfast, and it seems his associate found him afterward. This was found by his bed. If you would just sniff this, please."

She took the glass from him, the stem still in his handkerchief, and put her nose to it. "If you suspect poison, Professor, you're right. This bitter almond scent is one I've encountered before. Cyanide. You know, it's interesting that not everyone can catch the odor, as you did."

"How soon would death occur?" Bayard asked.

"From what I know—I've made rather a study of it since the murder investigation I was drawn into— cyanide can cause death in a minute or two, certainly no more than ten or fifteen minutes. A doctor could tell you more."

"None on the train, I'm afraid," Bayard said.

"You're our only expert, Miss Miller," Darnell added.

She frowned. "Well . . . cyanide is most likely swallowed, so the glass with the scent in it is consistent with that. As to symptoms? The victim gasps for breath, gets dizzy, and his pulse gets very rapid. He faints from a drop in his blood pressure. That's what happened in the case I mentioned. There may also be nausea."

"No indication of nausea," Darnell said, "and the Major would have been alone during his last minutes, according to Brand, so we don't know what symptoms he experienced."

"I could look at the body, if you wish."

"We're putting it off at the next station."

"Don't spies . . . I know he wasn't officially a spy, more of a messenger, according to what he said . . . but, don't they carry a poison pill? I've heard that."

Darnell nodded. "Brand said the Major did. But how could he be in danger of revealing secrets on this train? And if so, he'd just take the pill. No, someone else apparently slipped poison in his drink."

She studied the faces of the men. "So . . . it's murder?"

Bayard said to her, "That should not leave this room. Officially, I call it suicide. Only we three and Brand have this knowledge, and we must keep it that way."

She nodded.

They stepped out of her compartment and walked back to the caboose. The Express was slowing for its stop in Ulm. Darnell thought of the grisly cargo they had to dispatch and Madame Morgana's predictions and feelings of dread she expressed the night before. Was this death of a government courier the beginning of it all—the war the psychic predicted was coming soon?

The Orient Express chugged into the Ulm station just before noon. Bayard supervised the carrying of the Major's body by conductors from the caboose to a carriage and gave instructions to the local officials. Darnell and Penny stepped out onto the wooden platform and watched the proceedings from a distance. Curious workers and peasants also watched and whispered. Afterward, the locals milled about and marveled open-mouthed at the luxury of the train and the detrained passengers.

A newsboy came by offering Darnell a local paper.

Darnell shook his head. *"Nein, danke."* To Penny he said, "That's the extent of my German. I'm glad most people on this train speak English."

"Some speak the language of love." She looked into his eyes and smiled.

Darnell looked up and down the platform. Several passengers had stepped out for the exercise and fresh air. No one stood nearby. "I don't want to frighten you, Penny, but you must be careful from now on. Don't unlock our compartment door if I'm away unless you hear my voice."

"John, I know there's been a death—a suicide, you said. But you talk as if there's a murderer loose. What aren't you telling me?"

Darnell frowned. "What I'm saying now is the important thing. I rule nothing out. I take precautions, and you must, too."

The transfer of Major Coulton's body completed, Bayard gave signals to his conductors that the train would depart. The engineer gave a light tap on the whistle, a warning the train would be leaving.

Bayard approached Darnell and Penny. "This duty is finished. Time to board."

Rumors spread wildly through the train. Bryan Stark, the would-be aeronautical genius, had watched nervously from his window, as others had, as a large object wrapped in blankets, clearly a body, was unloaded. By lunchtime, the table talk was centered on only one topic—the Major's death.

Table partners for the Darnells' table included Bayard, Donald Brand, and the object of Brand's interest, Agatha Miller. Brand carried the Major's case, and secured it beneath his seat.

Agatha Miller looked into the young man's eyes. "I'm so sorry, Mr. Brand, about your companion.

Such a hearty man. Are you going on with your trip?"

"Of course. I must reach Bucharest. Unfortunately, I can't speak with anyone in authority, but I did talk with the local British consul, and he'll pass the word."

Penny said, "Agatha, my husband tells me you've had experience in this type of situation."

"Only a single case of the use of poison, but afterward I made a study of the subject. It may be useful in my books."

"Can you tell us about the case?"

The nurse nodded. "I was tending an older man in his home, a mansion really, on the outskirts of London. He had three children, all married, who lived in the city. The only other persons in the home were the servants. One morning the maid found him in his bed, dead."

"He had taken poison?" Penny spoke in a low voice.

"It was poison, yes. But Scotland Yard discovered it was not self-administered." She paused. "That's about all I can say. The family is well known."

Bayard said, "We mustn't let this deplorable case of suicide spoil our trip." He motioned to Chef Voisseron. "A bottle of your best Chablis." He turned to Darnell. "I'll visit the other tables, do some reassuring. Sample the wine for me if you will."

After lunch, Anton Donnelli sat beside Anna Held in his compartment. She stroked her Pomeranian and regarded Donnelli with a soft gaze. "You're very understanding, Anton."

"Sorrows are with us all. You must rebuild your life. It must be hard for you, your ex-husband, the great Florenz Ziegfeld, marrying that young girl last Saturday. He must be a man without a heart."

She rested a hand on his. "And you, Anton? Do you have a heart? I wonder about any man now." She thought of Philippe, whom she'd met in Paris in December. He would board at Budapest. Would she find herself choosing between the two of them?

Deep in her confused thoughts, she fingered the strands of pearls about her neck. She could thank Flo for those, and her other trinkets. Little enough to show for fifteen years. Could she find security with Anton, or Philippe? Or anyone?

Anton broke through her thoughts, touching her hand. "We have known each other less than a day, Anna, and I know you may have doubts. I want only to be your friend."

"You leave the train at Bucharest, as I do?"

"Yes. Business."

Anna smiled. "Does everything have to be mysterious on this train? Business, you say. But you don't tell me what business. Are you one of those spies?"

He laughed. "No, it's just that I can think only of you."

Anton put his arms around her. Anna felt the heat of his touch and knew instinctively she would be losing the reserve she had built around her since her divorce. She could be taking a step she could never retrace.

Anton leaned toward her and pressed his lips on hers, and she felt the thrill she had missed all those months since she left America. His hand roamed over her body, but she gave no resistance. At a critical moment, a knock came on the door.

Anton took a breath. "Who—who is it?"

"M'sieur Bayard and Professor Darnell. If we could talk for a moment?"

Anna pulled away from him, straightening her dress. "I should change." She rose and stepped over to the open connecting door of their compartments.

Donnelli stood and buttoned his coat. "After dinner, then, when it is more private . . . perhaps we have a nightcap here."

"Yes. Perhaps. Now I must go." She closed the door.

Anton Donnelli opened the corridor door and admitted the two men. He looked craftily from one to the other, wondering if they suspected his reputation as a thief. Had police caught up to him? Had they learned he was really Arturo Donatello using an alias?

The two visitors stood facing him as Donnelli took his seat by the window, to appear nonchalant, and lit a long, cylindrical cigar. "Cheroot?" He presented an open silver case lined with a dozen of the cigars.

They both declined. Bayard watched as Donnelli puffed contentedly. Darnell glanced about the room. Donnelli gasped as he noticed Anna's handkerchief lying on the sink, and covered the noise with a cough. Would the man see it?

"Nothing like a good smoke," Donnelli said. "Now, how can I help you—is it about that courier business?"

"You are very perceptive, m'sieur," Bayard said. "Your compartment adjoins that of the Major and Mr. Brand." He gestured in the direction opposite Anna Held's room. "These walls seem very thin in the quiet of the late hours of the night and early morning. We're wondering what you heard."

Donnelli breathed easier. They were not after him. He shook his head and puffed his cigar, which he found always gave him an air of suave innocence.

What man could be suspected when he was contentedly smoking a cigar in a relaxed manner?

He shook his head. "I have heard nothing. Perhaps some sounds, a door closing, but nothing unusual." He regarded the Manager. "I understand the Major took his own life."

"We're looking for indications of why he would do so."

Donnelli smiled, revealing white teeth seeming even more bright against his swarthy skin. "What makes any man give up life? Money, or lack of it. Or women." He scowled. "The fortunes of war, and of life." As he talked, memories of his earlier life renewed themselves—the scorned woman who turned him in to police as a burglary suspect, and his arrest in Belgrade. The six months he spent in the dank, dingy cell.

Darnell said, "A very philosophical attitude. You've observed men in these situations?"

"When you travel in Europe these days, you see surprising things. The world is changing very fast."

Bayard asked, "Did you have occasion to speak with the Major, or his assistant, last night or this morning?"

Donnelli saw a danger in getting involved. He would hold back what he knew. It seemed inconsequential enough. "No. I'm sorry, I can't help you." He stood, hoping they would take the signal and leave. He did not want to let something slip that he'd regret.

Bayard looked at Darnell. "Any other questions?"

"Not for now. We thank you, sir."

"We will see you at dinner, then," Bayard said. "You and your companion."

Donnelli closed the door after they left and leaned back against it. The Manager had referred to Anna

Held. Donnelli thought, Have I become too obvious with her? If her jewelry is found missing in Bucharest, he would not want to have undue attention drawn to himself. The Bucharest jails would be no better than those in Belgrade. And he wasn't a young man anymore.

Anton Donnelli stepped over to the sink and picked up Anna's handkerchief and held it up to catch its scent. Lilac. He wondered whether his emotions could stand in the way of his money needs this time. If so, it would be the first time.

Chapter Six

General Klaus Eberhardt, loyal always to Kaiser Wilhelm, nevertheless was impatient with his present assignment. He preferred the battlefield, fighting with men and guns, not the delicate duels with words in the inner sanctum sanctorums of state buildings in foreign governments.

He knew many were working to forestall the coming war, but for his part he found it difficult to wait for the first battles. After thirty years in the German army, and never having married, war and the conquest of beautiful women were his only desires. As to women, he preferred them to be exotic, with definite attitudes, a level of morals, and a mystery surrounding their activities that rivaled his own. Mata Hari, then, was a perfect match for him, and he for her.

He looked across the table at her and asked, "More champagne?" When she nodded, he refilled both of their glasses.

The dining car was empty except for the single waiter standing against the back wall, out of earshot, but alert for any motion for service from the General. It was that awkward time of afternoon, after lunch, but before the dinner hour. The British often filled it, the General reflected, with tea and cakes, and he expected some of them to arrive soon. He preferred a good German beer, or, when with a woman, the finest champagne.

"When war comes," he said, smiling, "the beer drinkers will beat the tea drinkers."

"You see war, then, with the British?" Mata Hari returned his smile.

"I cannot wait. I itch for the battle."

"And that itching—it brings you on this trip? Some conspiracies, some trading of loyalties with other countries?"

He could see that, despite the apparent commitment and convenience of their lustful liaisons at night, which continued a relationship established in Paris, she was always probing for information. She was the type of spy no one could trust. Was she working for the Germans now, or the French? Who could know? Regardless of his feelings for her—perhaps because of them, and his vulnerability—he knew he must be on his guard as to what he said and did.

"I do what you do, my dear. I carry out the wishes of my government. A good German soldier never asks why of his superiors, only how soon he must produce what they require of him."

Her dark eyes gazed into his, giving him that familiar feeling of uneasiness, almost as if she were peering at him through the sights of a rifle. "And what is required of you this time, Klaus? Treaties, armaments, oil? Would you hold that back from me?" She put her hand on his. "After all, we do know each other, shall I say . . . quite well."

"Love and war do not mix."

"Love! Ah, what a magnificent word, my General. So you love me, do you?" Her eyes were teasing.

Klaus Eberhardt grimaced. "All I know is I have a fever for you. Is that a symptom of love?"

"You, a man of the world, a General of the German Army, ask me that, a mere Folies Bergère dancer?" Her voice had a tantalizing lilt.

"Now you are really dangerous. Come, finish your champagne. We go to my compartment. To talk more of this."

"Yes," she laughed, "of course. To talk."

Prince Carol II of Rumania gazed at the passing landscape of Germany through the window of a compartment in his private salon car. The report of the Major's death, which had filtered forward into his cocoon of private luxury, disturbed him. Death on a train on which he was a virtual, although very comfortable, prisoner until he reached Bucharest was not within his plans.

As a young man of twenty-one, heir apparent to the throne of Rumania, he felt accustomed, indeed entitled, to having his every wish met simply upon command, having luxury without effort, and, certainly, enjoying comfort without risk. But now he felt a sense of very tangible impending danger.

For his comforts, he brought with him a court diplomat to attend him, Danya Petruso, and his Polish valet, Ludwik Mishenka. He brought also, as he did everywhere, his nominal secretary and de facto mistress, Zizi Lambrino, a voluptuous woman with long brown hair and contagious sexuality.

She was three years older than the Prince, but he saw this as no bar, and yearned to marry her, despite the social and royal conventions. As those close to him knew, her secretarial designation was not only for outward appearances, but primarily for the benefit of his critical father, the Crown Prince Ferdinand.

"Come here, Zizi. Sit beside me." Prince Carol motioned and patted the seat next to him.

She put aside a book and moved across the coach to his side. "Yes, my Prince."

His gaze found hers. "Many call me Prince, but from your lips, the word flows like a sip of wine."

Her laughter was musical, running up and down the scale. "You should be a poet. The poet Prince."

"And you should be my wife."

She frowned. "We've talked of that . . . but what would your father say? What would everyone say?" She clutched his arm. "You know I would be in heaven, but . . ."

He stopped her words with his lips on hers. After a long, tender kiss he said, "One day soon, Zizi, we will forget caution. We'll think of ourselves for once." His voice rose. "And I will marry you—in secret, if I must. But now, I have a problem."

"The death of the English Major?" She took his arm. "You must be careful. There may be a plot. You could be in danger. These trains are hotbeds for assassinations, or attempts."

He nodded. "I know. And I wonder about that suicide. With what I have to tell my father and the court on my return, some may wish to silence me."

"What will you do?" She looked at him with pleading eyes.

He mused. "There is a man aboard—a professor. The Manager has brought him on the train. This man is investigating certain matters."

"You will see him?"

When she said the words, Prince Carol's resolution firmed in his mind. "Yes. That is exactly what I must do. I'll see him tonight. At the dinner hour."

*   *   *

Anna Held regarded Madame Yolanda Morgana as the other woman took a seat beside her in Anna's compartment. Anna smiled and asked, "No crystal ball?"

The Madame shook her head and scowled. "That particular device—it is to convince the unitiated of a psychic's power. To impress them."

"And what are your powers? You say you can see into the future. You predict events for entire countries—can you do that also for the solitary human being? For a woman, like myself?"

The Madame took Anna Held's hands in hers. "Do not question so much, my dear lady. Relax your thoughts, so they become accessible. Relax your body and your mind. Relax completely. Close your eyes."

The actress nodded and closed her eyes, still holding the hands of the Madame.

"Remove the blocks to your concentration," Madame Morgana intoned in a monotonous voice. "Remove the walls that protect you from the hard world about you, the walls that keep others from seeing how you feel, what you are, where you are going." Her soft voice sounded in a monotone, moving up and down only slightly in a close range, the phrases rising and falling rhythmically. "Now you feel relaxed, very relaxed; your arms feel heavy; they are very heavy; they drop to your lap; your body is slack; your legs are like warm wax."

Anna's arms fell to her lap as Morgana released them. She slumped back against her seat, eyes still closed. Her breathing became deep and heavy.

"You are asleep, now, but are aware of my voice. You will respond to my voice, and my voice only. And when I later say the word 'awake' you will awake refreshed and will recall nothing of our conversation. Do you understand this?"

"Yes."

"Now, open your eyes and look at me."

Anna opened her eyes. She stared at the psychic.

"Tell me about your marriage, and why it ended."

Deep creases formed between Anna's eyes. "Divorce. My divorce. He threw me aside for younger actresses. Then I divorced him."

"Who were they?"

"There were two of them."

"Stars?"

"No, young things. Ingenues."

"You hated him, and the women?"

"Yes." She frowned more deeply.

"You have met other men—since then?"

"Yes."

"Tell me about them. Tell me about the first man you met."

Anna's eyes stared ahead unseeingly. "Philippe. We met in Paris. He travels. He will board in Vienna."

"Do you love Philippe?"

"I—I don't know. He is rich."

"Then security is what you want?"

Tears came into Anna's eyes. "Yes. I must have it. I cannot act on the stage any longer."

"Why?"

"I am forty-one. The audience wants girls in their twenties."

"You have lost confidence?"

"Yes."

"Who else have you met, what other man?"

"On the train, next to me. Anton."

"And how do you feel about Anton?"

"I don't know. There is warmth, fire."

"Love?"

"I don't know." Anna twisted in her seat.

"Be relaxed. Relax."

Anna's facial muscles relaxed. The deeper frown lines left her forehead.

"Which of these men will you choose?"

"I must have money. I have none."

"Philippe?"

"Oh, I can't tell you, I can't tell you . . ." Anna's voice rose, and she squirmed and twisted her hands together.

"All right, all right." The voice was soothing, syrupy. "You are fully relaxed. Close your eyes again. You will soon be able to reach your decision. You will decide based on what is in your heart. Now, in a moment, when I say the word, you will awake refreshed and happy, unaware of our talk, undisturbed by your thoughts. Now . . . awake!"

Anna's eyes opened and she took a deep breath. "Oh—did I fall asleep?"

"My dear lady, you were in a somnolent state, a trance."

"You . . . mesmerized me?"

"When we talked last night, I told you of that possibility. I did not know until I tried whether you would go under. You did, and you are perfectly fine now."

"So, you talked with me? You found out something about my future?"

Madame Morgana stared out the window at the passing fields and wooded areas of the German landscape. "The glass of the future is always cloudy, but the signposts are sometimes easy to read. We face crossroads which can take us in one direction or the other."

"That is where I am, at a crossroads."

"Often we do not know which road we should take until we reach that junction. But our hidden minds, the custodians of our souls, point the way."

"But me? What will happen to me?"

"You will know what to do when the time comes. But, if you want to know more—show me your palm, dear lady. Your right hand, please."

Madame Morgana took Anna's hand in hers and gazed at the lines in her palm. She traced them with her finger. "A deep love line. It is broken, and shows your heartaches. The head line is strong. The life line . . ." She frowned and released Anna's hand.

"What is it?" Anna searched the Madame's face for expression.

"It is nothing, nothing. I am tired now."

"Tell me more, please."

Madame Morgana nodded. "We will talk again before Budapest. But I can tell you this—I believe you will make an important choice before this journey ends. You will think of your future and decide upon a course of action. And it will be the best for you. You have nothing to fear from your choice." She stood. "Now I must go."

Outside the corridor, after Anna closed the door behind her, Madame Morgana shook her head and walked toward the second car and her own compartment. "A few years . . . poor woman."

She thought of the irony of Anna Held, wanting security so badly, but needing it for such a short time.

Inside her compartment, the Madame leaned back against the door. She closed her eyes and rubbed her temples.

"I must be wrong," the Madame said aloud, but in a whisper. She stepped to the sink and poured brandy into a glass from a silver flask in her bag. She raised the glass. "To you, Anna Held. I hope I'm wrong about your life. You deserve better than that."

Chapter Seven

While Penny was at the water closet at the end of the corridor, Darnell stepped over to the next compartment and rapped on the door. Tony Arnaud opened it.

Darnell glanced into the room and saw Elizabeth Arnaud at the table. "May I come in for a moment?"

Arnaud waved a hand. "Please. It is Professor, *n'est-ce pas?*"

Darnell nodded. "Have you had any more experiences with the apparition?"

Elizabeth smiled at him from across the room. "No. Nothing. And I'm glad. Once is enough."

"You realize I'm ready to do anything if it does occur? I'm right next door in compartment eight."

Tony Arnaud said, "You investigate these kinds of matters, is it not so? How can you investigate a ghost?"

"Based on experience, I observe and study. May I inspect?"

Arnaud spread his arms. *"Certainment."*

Darnell walked slowly about the room looking for anything at all remarkable. Most of their belongings were still in their suitcases. He peered into a cupboard, a drawer, and a closet. He shook his head. "I see nothing to call for investigation."

Arnaud shook his hand. "Thank you for coming over."

Darnell nodded good-bye to Elizabeth and left the room.

Back in his own compartment, he reflected upon the couple. Young, especially the woman. In his experience the very young and the very old were the most susceptible to bizarre experiences of this sort. It was a matter of innocent belief.

Penny Darnell returned from the water closet in her robe, her hair wet, her cheeks glowing from the scrubbing she'd given them. "I feel much better now. Getting the grit off. I swear, the soot from the engine comes right in through the windows."

"Maybe this rain will clean off the soot." Darnell nodded toward the window, where slants of raindrops had begun beating against the glass in a rat-a-tat rhythm, driven partly by the wind, partly by the force of the train's speed.

"Well, we won't be able to take our afternoon walk in the park," she laughed. Then, with a small frown, she said, "I do miss walking. These train trips are so confining."

"We'll walk to the dining car soon." He took her in his arms and felt the wetness of her hair against his neck. "Or, we could just . . ."

Penny laughed. "I'm hungry. So get dressed. I'll do the same." She threw her robe on the seat and stepped over to her suitcase.

Darnell watched her, and sighed.

The string quartet played a spirited Mozart piece. General Eberhardt and Mata Hari—Margaret Zelle to everyone on the train except Eberhardt—already sat at their appointed table when Darnell and Penny arrived. Following them, Pierre Bayard said, "I'll join you in a moment, after I make the rounds." Madame Morgana approached the table and took a seat opposite Penny.

Darnell said, "Our pleasure to have you join us, General. I enjoyed our talk about politics last night. Miss Zelle, happy you're here. You've met my wife, Penny, and the Madame."

Eberhardt said, "*Danke schön*—Margaret and I thank you. We sit where M'sieur Bayard places us. It is good to meet all those on the Express." He glared pointedly at the Turks and Greeks at their table, beginning their usual loud conversation and laughter. "With a few exceptions," he added.

Darnell laughed. "Perhaps we're just too serious."

Madame Morgana sniffed. "This train is not one for gaiety. We already have had one death. There may be more."

General Eberhardt turned to her. "Do not be so full of gloom, Madame. You write of your fears for the war. But war refreshes the soul, renews the patriotism, clears the air."

She sniffed. "The air of Europe will be filled with smoke, it will reverberate with cannon fire, it will smell of death." Morgana stared in the General's eyes. "The first blush of the glamour of war will seem pale compared with the blood of the young who die."

The General smiled. "I know the saying, 'If the old men had to fight the wars, there would be no wars.' But I am not eighteen. And I am ready to fight."

"Fight whom?" Darnell challenged. "Are you choosing sides already?"

"No, no. I'm speaking theoretically, of course. Germany has no enemies. But friends can become antagonists when you least expect it. Sometimes over trifles, sometimes . . . more."

The waiter brought menus, took wine orders, and set plates of fresh vegetable crudités and fruit on the table. In moments, Chef Voisseron appeared with two bottles of red wine. The Chef skillfully opened them and poured a bit into his small tasting cup. He sampled it. "Ah, excellent." He poured a small quantity in Eberhardt's glass. "General? Do you approve?"

The General sipped it and nodded. "Not German, but good." The Chef filled all the glasses and went on to the next table.

Penny said, "Can we speak of something more pleasant?" She looked at Mata Hari. "Miss Zelle—I understand you're a dancer."

Mata Hari nodded. "But I am not a Pavlova—I don't dance on my toes." She smiled. "I've danced privately, in clubs, and had several seasons in the *Folies Bergère*. Of course, I create my own dances."

"Do you perform the new South American dance—the tango?"

"Not on stage. One of my dances involves many large veils, which I remove one by one. I dance to the night, to the morning, to the moon, to the sun."

Madame Morgana studied her more closely now, her eyes narrowing. She spoke softly, "To the eye of the day."

Mata Hari, startled, looked from the Madame to the General. He frowned, and shook his head, as if to tell her, *Say nothing in response.*

The food came, saving the moment.

Penny thought, That moment seemed difficult for the dancer. But she wondered now if there was more to this dancer than she revealed. Did the Madame divine something more, did she have that power, too? Penny hooked her arm in Darnell's as they watched the waiter ladle soup into their bowls.

The meal progressed quickly this night. Soup was followed by a fish course, roast beef with fresh vegetables, a light green salad. And, finally, a dessert cart was brought around.

As the last dessert was being served, the door opened and Prince Carol stood in the doorway, his secretary by his side. He stepped forward into the car and walked slowly, Zizi Lambrino following, toward the table where Bayard sat. The Manager rose and came out to the aisle to greet his royal passenger.

The Prince acknowledged Bayard's deep bow and asked, "A champagne glass? And for Miss Lambrino? I would make a toast."

Bayard stepped quickly to a serving table and filled two fluted glasses from an open champagne bottle and handed them to the Prince and his secretary.

"I salute you all," Prince Carol said. "Let us drink to our journey together on the *Orient Express*." He raised his glass and looked about the room, letting his gaze rest on each in turn. The others raised their glasses and spoke various salutations.

Afterwards, when the buzz of conversation resumed, the Prince motioned Bayard to come to his side. "I'd be pleased if you and Professor Darnell would join me in my salon car after your meal."

The Manager moved his head up and down vigorously and looked at Darnell, who had heard the request. Darnell nodded.

"We'll be there," Bayard said.

When the meal was finished, several of the men adjourned to the smoking salon for brandy and war talk, while some women, including Penny, went to the ladies' salon to sip tea and enjoy lighter conversation. Bayard and Darnell walked forward to the Prince's private salon car.

Bryan Stark, one thing only on his mind, the possible sale of the aircraft plans, saw General Eberhardt's lady companion heading toward the ladies' salon with the other women, and the General going to his compartment. He decided this might be his one chance. He followed the General to his room, waited a moment, and rapped on the door. It opened at once and the General stared at him with cold fish-eyes.

"General . . . Eberhardt, I believe?" Stark spoke hesitantly in the presence of the imposing, uniformed man with a stern expression.

"Yes. What is it?"

"I am Bryan Stark. You may have seen me dining?"

"Yes. You keep to yourself, don't you?"

"With good reason. I have something you may be interested in. May I come in?"

Eberhardt's eyes narrowed. "I do not see . . . all right, for a few minutes."

After Stark entered, the General closed the door. "You're selling something? You are a salesman, yes?"

Stark gave him a twisted smile. "In a manner of speaking."

The General motioned to the table, and the two sat opposite each other. "Very well," the General said, "I do not have much time."

"Aviation," Stark said, "is in the vanguard of progress for the rest of this century. Nations will depend on it." He paused.

"Go on. I am interested."

"What would it be worth to you, to your country and your military people, General, to obtain plans for a prototype of a new aircraft, that could be a fighting plane, one with remarkable, advanced engineering?"

"A prototype? Meaning?"

"A model. The first of its kind. I believe it will lead the way for all future single-seater combat planes."

"It is a fighter plane?"

"Yes."

"And you have the plans of the plane? They are your plans?"

"I possess them."

General Eberhardt smiled. "So—you are a salesman, after all. You avoid the issue of ownership. But the price?"

"I ask *you* that—what would it be worth to your government?"

Eberhardt stared into Stark's eyes and said, "Do not be naive. I would have to see them. Show them to me—and I will tell you."

The young man felt the force of the other's personality, and the power in his gaze and words. He looked down to gather his strength. This was harder than he'd thought. Was he crazy to talk with a German general?

"I will show you enough of the plans to convince you. But we must do this before we reach Budapest." Stark glanced at the General's connecting door, which he knew led to the room of the woman he heard called Miss Margaret Zelle, whom the General was with constantly. "It would be more private if you came to my compartment."

"The woman is not a problem—but, yes, I will come to your room. I will let you know." He pulled out his watch. "Now you must go."

Prince Carol greeted Bayard and Darnell with the youthful enthusiasm and directness of his twenty-one years. "What I must know, gentlemen, is whether I am in personal danger, whether the heir to the crown of Rumania—myself—could be harmed or killed. M'sieur Bayard?" He motioned to chairs, inviting Bayard and Darnell to seat themselves opposite him.

Bayard bowed from the waist. "Professor Darnell and I do understand your concern. But first, let me say we are calling the death of Major Coulton a suicide."

"Calling it?" The Prince's heavy eyebrows arched upward, as did his tone of voice. "That sounds vague."

"Well, . . . Professor?" Bayard turned to him.

Darnell leveled his gaze at the young Prince. "Your Highness, we must be honest with you. The Major had the potential for suicide—a pill, that last resort measure that senior couriers have. It's an escape device, in case they are in danger of revealing critical state secrets. It's possible he took such a pill."

"But it's also possible . . . ?"

"That it was murder." Darnell was pleased to see the young man did not flinch at the word.

Prince Carol looked from one of them to the other. "Then we'll say murder, the worst case. A spy is murdered by someone on the train. Who will be next? What are you doing about it?"

Darnell said, "There are many questions, Prince Carol. If there is a murderer aboard, that person cannot leave the train. There could be more violence, if there is a more insidious plot. But what I must ask is, do you have any reason—any special reason—for feeling this violence could reach into your salon car and affect you? We need your help on that point."

"You are very perceptive, Professor. I tell you and the Manager this in confidence. I am carrying information back to my father's court that may be critical to our country if war comes."

"Someone could want to suppress that."

"Right. Europe is boiling for war. The balance among the Great Powers is delicate, and if two go to war, six will follow, which will become ten. Within each nation, people speak of their country's honor, safety, and future. There are cultural forces at work, religious and race antagonism. There will be a fight to the finish."

"France has a three-year draft," Bayard said.

"Exactly. And Germany's armies are a third larger than they were just a few years ago. Europe is armed for peace, they say. But it will all end in war. What irony!"

Darnell said, "Some talk of taking sides, already. As if battle plans are in existence."

The Prince nodded. "All that is needed is one spark to start the flames. No one knows when that spark will be ignited."

"The immediate question is your safety," Darnell said. "You have two men in your car. They can help in shielding you. Your car can be, and should be, locked at all times. We will station a conductor to watch the doors."

"Poison," the Prince said, "can be administered in food. Do I need a food taster?"

Bayard sat silently for a moment. "I will have Chef Voisseron prepare all of the food for everyone in your royal car personally. All your wines will be delivered into your car unopened, and the Chef will open them for you—and he always tastes all wine."

Prince Carol nodded. "Good. That is satisfactory. Now, one more thing. Professor—the apparition we hear about. There are rumors."

"Rumors do abound," Darnell answered. "One of

M'sieur Bayard's passengers felt she saw an apparition. In her mind, that's what it was. She may have seen nothing—dreams, imagination, and the power of suggestion are strong forces. But in any case, we know of no connection between that sighting, valid or not, and the Major's death. And that matter should be of no concern to you, although we'll continue to study it."

The Prince stood. "Well, then, I thank you both. We begin the new food and drink regimen immediately, M'sieur Bayard?"

"Yes. At once." He and Darnell stood, the Manager bowed, and the two took their leave. Standing outside the door, they heard the bolt thrown.

"Good," Darnell said. "He's locked in for the night."

"It's after eleven," Bayard said. "I'll make the rounds one more time."

"And I'll pick up Penny at the ladies' salon."

All passengers retired earlier that night, reflecting the tiring trip and dampening influence of Major Coulton's death. The suicide diminished the spirit of adventure. Madame Morgana's forewarnings of gloom seemed self-fulfilling, subtly changing the atmosphere. The Prince's changes in routine put it all in perspective—not even a Prince could be completely safe.

As Darnell walked to his compartment with Penny, he reflected that one could say the train was under siege, perhaps in reality, certainly in perception. And it was under siege not from without the train, but from within.

Chapter Eight

The continuing rainstorm slowed the train's progress as it pushed forward on the long stretch from Munich to Vienna, and time had been lost at Ulm delivering Major Coulton's body to the authorities. It would not reach Vienna until early morning.

Only ambient light through the window relieved the darkness in the Darnells' compartment. Penny faced the bed. She wore a delicate pink nightgown and swayed back and forth, her body undulating from side to side to a tune she softly hummed. She smiled at Darnell sloe-eyed.

Darnell stretched his arms out to her. "Come here," he said, with a smile, feigning a foreign accent. "I vant you in mine arms, you exciting creature."

Penny moved to the bed and lay in his arms. "Ummm. A delayed honeymoon with you is really something—a ghost, a suicide, and now a Prince."

After a moment, she said, "Tell me about the Prince, John. What did he want? And don't hold back on me."

Darnell smiled, smoothing her hair back gently, saying in an accent, "Vould I hold back from mine bride?"

"You're doing it now—not answering. You know

more ways how *not* to answer a question than I do to ask it. C'mon." She frowned and dug a finger into his ribs.

"Some things are in confidence."

"Now!" She pinched his side, and her violet eyes flashed.

He laughed. "All right. The Prince is worried about himself. If the Major's death turns out to be murder . . ."

"Murder—"

"I told you. I rule nothing out. Prince Carol's worried he could be next. He wants someone to taste his food for poison."

"That's an important job—but it might not have much future."

"He's a Prince. Food tasting is an old custom for royalty."

"John, honestly, do you think the Major was murdered?"

"All I can say is, it is a possibility. Officially, Bayard calls it suicide. Reports of a murder aboard the train . . . he can't face that. But I have to proceed as if it *was* murder. So the Prince is locked in for the night."

Penny pushed hair back from his forehead. "And so are we."

Tony Arnaud felt good about the situation he found himself in, with a beautiful new wife, a honeymoon, free transport all the way to their destination in Greece, and the Orient Express to enjoy. Yet, in one respect, he felt guilty. Just a month ago he was wondering where he could sell a painting to help pay the rent of his Left Bank studio in Paris. Then he met Elizabeth Hopkins, and his world changed. But gnawing at his conscience was his feeling that he was taking advantage of her, and the train line.

"You . . . you do love me, Elizabeth?" His insecurity showed in his hesitant voice.

"Tony! What a question. Of course I do. What's bothering you—the money I took from Father?"

"Maybe that. I'm making you do things that are not right."

"Nonsense. Father will never miss the money."

"And the train—getting free fares, because of what you saw."

She touched his hand. "The manager offered it. It was his suggestion. You simply agreed."

"And the ghost? It bothers you no more?"

"I'm over that. What it was, I'll never know, but it doesn't matter now. Don't worry about that anymore."

"Another thing, your father. I don't want him to think I am after his money—*your* money." His brows creased deeply and he looked down.

Elizabeth sat beside him on the bed. "You're worrying too much, Tony. You need some good news. There's something, well, very special I have to tell you."

He looked up at her. *"Oui?"*

"Yes," she laughed. *"Very* wee."

He frowned. "I don't know . . . You mean, what?"

"Remember how we got carried away that night in Paris—love at first sight? Five weeks before our wedding yesterday?"

"Oui—I mean, yes."

"It's all right to speak French. You can teach our son—or daughter—your language." She looked at him with twinkling eyes.

"Son? Daughter? I don't . . . You're . . . ?"

She nodded, smiling. "We're going to have a child, Tony. At least I think so. If what they tell me . . ."

Tony Arnaud swept her into his arms. Then he pulled back. "Do I hurt you?"

She laughed. "No. No danger of that, yet."

"So this train, our elopement, even with our ghost—they bring us good luck."

Elizabeth nodded. "We'll enjoy our honeymoon trip, and then go right to London and tell Father and Mother. When they hear they'll be having a grandchild, nothing else will matter."

"The Grand Hotel," Mata Hari said, musing, as she stared out the train window at the passing fields and trees and the occasional farmhouse light in the distance. "It was a fateful meeting place." The steady, unrelenting roar of the train's engine and the revolutions of the wheels had put her in a reflective mood. She thought of Paris, how she had taken leave of her dance obligations for this trip, how she had met the General at the hotel and learned he was taking the same train, and of what had happened since.

There was a comfortable familiarity in her relationship with the General, and a not altogether pleasant or unpleasant sameness—more than she had found in her other affairs. Yet she yearned for genuine affection, and felt she could never find it. She took what she could get. What was the German word? *Ersatz.* Imitation of love. Lust, at best.

The General looked up from the papers he was studying. "Grand Hotel? Yes, we had an excellent time there, did we not?" But now he studied her.

"Don't stare at me, Klaus. You make me feel, sometimes, like I'm a target on your firing range." She twisted her fingers together and unwound them in what she knew was a nervous habit.

"Yes. You are my target. Of love."

She scowled. "There is that word, again. A word with no meaning in these times."

"You would prefer the word 'war'? That would have real meaning?" He set his papers aside, upside down.

"It would have reality. My life needs reality. It needs a goal. I can't dance forever. In a few years I'll be forty."

Klaus Eberhardt moved to her side and put an arm around her shoulders. "You want comfort, my dear, protection, and security. That is why you are with a German General. Why your instinct picked me from that group in the bar." He touched his lips to hers. After a moment, he said, "We have this time, *liebfrau*, this moment. That is all anyone ever really has."

Mata Hari looked at him with tears in her eyes. "Then let us have the wine. To celebrate this moment—all that we have."

They sipped their wine in the dark room, in each other's arms. The train noises blended with the heavy, even breathing of the General, who succumbed to the effects of his too-heavy meal, the after-dinner drinks, and now the wine. He soon fell asleep.

Mata Hari extricated herself from his arms and rose from the bed. She carefully arranged the wine bottle and his glass on the window ledge, knowing he would wake in an hour or two and want more to drink, as was his custom. She picked up the papers he had been studying, crossed the room, and stepped into her own compartment, pulling the connecting door closed as she entered. She bolted the door, clicked on the bed light, and spread the papers out on her bed.

Pierre Bayard rose early to be alert when they reached Vienna at six a.m. Only three passengers were due to board. Since the main car was full, they would be booked into the second car, in which his own room was situated. They would ride in comfort, if not luxury. He stood at the open door, and, as the train slowed, he stepped down to the platform, moving in the forward direction of the train.

When the train stopped, several persons came forward. "I am Philippe Cuvier," said a tall man in a homburg hat, striped suit, and cream-colored vest. "The train is late." He made a show of checking his gold watch. "You are the Manager?"

Bayard nodded. "At your service."

"Then you can find me Miss Anna Held. She is on the train?"

"Yes." Bayard sized up the man. He was a bit imperious. And Bayard knew he could offer the excuse of the woman's privacy. "If you would wait until the breakfast call at eight, she will be in the dining room."

The man glanced at his watch. "Yes. That will suffice."

Bayard directed a conductor to take Cuvier to his compartment. He watched him swagger off, and then assigned conductors to accompany the others boarding.

After the quick boarding, Bayard thought of returning to his own quarters. But he saw a woman, Margaret Zelle, her nightgown and robe flapping loosely around her and her hair in disarray, running toward him down the corridor.

"Oh! M'sieur Bayard, you must come with me. Quickly!"

She grabbed his arm and turned back down the corridor, moving fast, halfway between a walk and a run, pulling him along behind her. "It's the General. You must see to him. He's had a fit, or something."

She reached the General's compartment door, which was standing open, and rushed into the room. She pointed at General Klaus Eberhardt, sprawled on his bed. A bottle and glass lay on the floor next to it.

The General groaned. His wide eyes stared at the ceiling.

"It may be his heart," she said.

Bayard said, "Water. Pour some water. And get some brandy." He helped the General into a sitting position. He glanced at the open connecting door between the General's compartment and the one beyond, the room assigned to her. "Put a cold cloth on his head, Miss Zelle. Don't touch anything. I will be back in two minutes."

He hurried to the end of the car and knocked loudly on the door of John Darnell's compartment. There was no answer and he knocked again, more loudly.

The door opened and John Darnell looked out at him. "What? Oh, Pierre? What is it?" He stifled a yawn.

"Professor! We have another problem. Go to the General's compartment. I'll meet you there."

Darnell turned and looked back into the room. Penny peered at him.

"I'll change." He looked down at his pajamas.

"Grab a robe, pants. Hurry."

Darnell closed the door and, after explaining briefly to Penny, he emerged in a minute wearing slippers, pants, and his Chinese silk robe. He hurried toward the General's compartment.

Bayard retraced his steps rapidly down the corridor. He met the conductor, Albert, and said, "Wake Miss Miller and bring her to the General's room, immediately." He pushed open the door to the General's compartment, just as Darnell arrived, and followed him into the room. Margaret Zelle rose as they entered.

Darnell went to the General. "How are you feeling?" He held the man's wrist to feel his pulse. "Rapid," he said to Bayard. He picked up the bottle of wine and the glass from the floor with a handkerchief and sniffed of the liquid in them.

Agatha Miller knocked and entered the compartment. "Albert said you wanted me . . ." she began, then saw the General sitting on the bed. She exchanged a glance with Darnell. "Another . . . incident?" She stepped forward to the bed.

Bayard bit a fingernail and looked at her and Darnell. "I can't take much more of this, Professor."

"Easy, Pierre," Darnell said. "Look him over, Miss Miller, please."

The nurse stepped forward and peered at the General's pink face. "There's an odor of cyanide on his nightshirt from spillage of his drink. Apparently he didn't drink more than a taste." She glanced at the sink. "Lost it in here."

"Thank God," Mata Hari said.

Darnell said, "There are traces of it in the bottle and glass."

"I've never been so sick," General Eberhardt said.

Bayard groaned. He held his head in his hands and leaned forward, his head down.

"Are you all right?" Agatha asked. "Some water . . . ?"

He waved his hand. "No, no, I'm just thinking of telling my passengers. Another poisoning."

"I know," Darnell said. "But wait a bit. I have some questions to ask Miss Zelle."

The nurse gave brandy to the General. "Drink this."

Darnell looked at Mata Hari, whose gaze met his steadily.

"You were in the General's compartment last night, Miss Zelle. Tell us what transpired, please."

She nodded. "After dinner, I opened my connecting door to his room. We had wine in here, and talked. That's all. He fell asleep, and I went back to my room and closed the door. When I . . . came back in this morning, I found him like this, and went to fetch Mr. Bayard." She frowned. "I think that's all."

"You and the General are traveling together?"

"Not really. I met him in Paris. We had both booked the Express to Bucharest, and he asked for connecting rooms."

"Coincidence, then. But finding yourselves here, you spent time together?"

She nodded. "I enjoyed his company. Train rides can be boring when you're alone."

Darnell gazed directly into her dark eyes. "Don't you think it's time to drop your pretense?"

"Pretense?" She drew her robe around her.

Agatha Miller looked at Darnell, eyebrows raised. Bayard's mouth stood open.

"Yes. Wouldn't it be more appropriate now, instead of Margaret Zelle, to use your stage name of Mata Hari?"

Bayard gasped.

Agatha Miller, with wide eyes, turned her attention to the woman.

Mata Hari smiled. "So you've found me out, Professor. But it's really no great mystery. You can see by the reaction of these two," she said, gesturing sweepingly at Bayard and the nurse, "that my mere name, Mata Hari, causes a sensation. I have no privacy at all when I use that name. So I travel under my real name, Margaret Zelle. Or, as my father baptized me, Margaretha." Her forehead creased. "But . . . how did you find out?"

Darnell dismissed her question with a gesture. "Simple enough. At dinner tonight, you spoke of dancing 'to the morning, to the sun.' Madame Morgana said the odd words, 'To the eye of the day.' She had focused on you, with her keen mind, and pierced your secret. Then I remembered, from all of your publicity releases and stories—Mata, the sun, or the eye—and Hari, the day. From the Malayan language. 'The eye of the day.'"

She nodded. "It's true. I lived in Malay for some years with my husband." She shook her head. "Very bad memories from there—my son died, when he was just a child. But I took my stage name from their language."

"You must know more about this matter."

She shook her head. "No. But I am glad he's alive." She put her arm around the General's shoulder. "People seem to die around me. I'm glad he didn't."

"Was his door to the corridor locked?"

"I don't know. I came in here through my connecting door and ran out through his corridor door."

Darnell turned to Bayard. "Do you recall, Pierre?"

He stared into space, frowning. "When she came for me and we ran back here, the door was standing open."

Mata Hari nodded. "Yes. When I found the General in his condition, I ran out through his door, naturally. I must have left it open when I went looking for the Manager."

"It wasn't bolted on the inside when you left?"

"Definitely not bolted. And it might have been unlocked. I couldn't tell. It opened to my touch. I wasn't thinking of locks."

"So, the door was not bolted," Darnell said grimly. "And if someone attempted to murder him, we've managed to narrow it down to simply everyone on the train.''

Bayard groaned again. He stood, and they prepared to leave.

The nurse said, "Just give him plenty of water, miss. Stay with him. We'll look in again later.''

In the corridor, the General's door shut behind them, Agatha Miller said, "I'm sure you don't see this one as a suicide attempt.''

Darnell shook his head. "Right. We have to assume this was an attempt at murder. But nothing is clear. What we thought we knew in Coulton's case is now colored by this one. In some strange way, they have to be connected.''

"The poison is one connection.''

He nodded, then said, "You should keep the name Mata Hari confidential.''

"Naturally,'' Agatha Miller said, as she turned to leave for her room. "But she'll have to face the spotlight sometime—it's the price of fame.''

Chapter Nine

When Agatha Miller walked off, Albert approached the two men. Darnell sensed that the conductor, who untypically held his cap in his hands, had something important on his mind. "You have something to tell us, Albert?"

"Ye-es, sir." He looked to Bayard for confirmation.

"*Mon Dieu!* Speak up, man." Bayard glared down at the short man, his gaze almost parallel with the top of his bald head. "And put your cap back on."

The conductor replaced his cap, which he had been twisting in his fingers. "I-I delivered something to the General last night. I thought . . ."

Darnell gestured with a hand. "Come, tell us what you thought."

"I thought you ought to know of the sleeping powders. I brought them here last night."

"You gave them to the General?" Darnell looked sidelong at Bayard, whose mouth was open.

"No. I set them on the sink near a glass. I thought he would take them later."

"The time?"

"About eleven, just after he returned to his compartment."

"He was alone?"

"Yes."

"And the source of these powders?"

"In the storeroom. A large jar. I dipped out a portion, one large scoop."

"Thank you, Albert." Darnell dismissed him with a salute. "You've done your duty."

The conductor walked down the corridor to his post and sat on the stool in the corner.

"Another complication," Bayard said.

"Right. Cyanide is often in powder form."

"I think I'd better confiscate that jar."

"Secure it," Darnell said. "But contact the Vienna police first. They should investigate officially. We're still at the station, so that's convenient."

"Oh, my God. Another delay."

Darnell rested a hand on Bayard's shoulder. "Fortunately, the General is still with us, there's no death involved. Their questions may not take long. But they must be asked into this."

Darnell returned to his compartment, to Penny, now awake, who was staring out the window at police approaching the train.

"What's happening, John?"

"An apparent attempt on the General's life. Or—if one wants to be more devious—a heart attack."

She smiled. "I suspect we poor passengers are going to be fed the heart attack line, like the Coulton suicide story."

He sat beside her on the bed and stroked her bare arms. "Poor passengers, indeed—such poor surroundings, such poor food."

She frowned daintily. "You know what I mean. Now, stop being difficult, and kiss me good morning. I've never been kissed in Vienna before."

Twenty minutes later they were on their way to

the dining car, when Albert came hurrying down the corridor, breathing hard. "The Prince," he gasped. "He wishes to see you, Professor. Now."

Darnell took Penny's hand and said, "You're coming with me this time. I'm not sure I want to let you out of my sight unless you're locked in our room. And it's time you met the Prince."

They walked through the dining car and the car containing the men's and ladies' salons, and reached the Prince's private car. Darnell knocked on the door. A face showed through the glass window, and the Prince's valet opened the door.

"Ludwik Mishenka at your service. The Prince is waiting inside." He gave them a short, abrupt bow, stood aside as they entered, and bolted the door again after they walked by him. "Straight ahead," he said.

The Prince sat at a table by the window. Seeing Penny with Darnell, he rose and bowed. "Madame Darnell," he said. "A pleasure." He reached out smoothly and took her hand in his. He made a gesture of kissing the air about an inch from her hand, then abruptly dropped it. "Please, sit down."

They took seats opposite him. He motioned out the window at green-coated officers. "The *gendarmes*. Please explain this."

Darnell nodded. "You like directness, Your Highness. It appears that General Eberhardt narrowly escaped death."

"And the source of that danger?"

"One might say a heart attack. Another might say an aborted poisoning attempt."

"I knew it!" The Prince smashed a fist into his open palm. "There is a plot aboard this train. A plot to kill me."

Darnell returned the glare of the young Prince's

eyes into his own. "If you have particulars, Prince Carol, it would help our investigation. Is there someone you suspect? Someone we should, perhaps, interrogate?"

"No, no. But there are things you must know. They might help."

"You mentioned you're carrying information back to your father and his court. Information that may affect the war." Darnell studied the Prince's face, wondering if he could detect a lie from the young man's mouth.

The Prince spoke in a lowered voice. "No one in this car, no one east of Berlin in fact, knows this. I have spoken with those in the highest authority in Germany. They wish to sign a treaty with Rumania to secure use of our oil reserves—our oil fields in fact—in return for a nonaggression pact. But this is what's important—I also have offers from the British. My father must answer both within thirty days, every day counts."

"Why is it so urgent?"

Prince Carol shook his head. "I don't mean to say that war is coming in thirty days. Just that we must prepare ourselves."

"And if you don't deliver the message, and outline the offers to your father?"

His forehead creased and the Prince answered slowly. "Our country could find itself under attack, and lose its oil in any case."

"You fear attack by Germany?"

"Exactly."

"So—those who would wish to stop your mouth—excuse my words—would be whom?"

"Germans themselves, I'm afraid. Those who don't want the British message to go through, who know

I don't trust them, and their pieces of paper. I prefer the British and French."

"Any others who have an interest?"

"I would not eliminate the Turks. They're in the middle, caught in a spiderweb of intrigue, and want to negotiate their way out of the web. The Pashas operate behind the scenes."

Penny asked, "Who—I mean, Your Highness . . . who are the Pashas?"

Prince Carol smiled, and his clear blue eyes fixed on Penny's. "I know you're from America, and I don't expect every nuance of courtesy from Americans. You have no royalty there, other than your monied class." He paused. "The Pashas are like the elder statesmen of their land. Hakki Pasha is their main negotiator, a former Grand Vizier. He's still in Paris."

Darnell said, "New treaties for a coming war?"

"No doubt—the Turks' German military attaché is in Berlin. Some others are the elder negotiator Heggar Pasha, also a Vizier. And Ovar Pasha, who is close to the general command in both France and Germany because of his military connections."

"They could gain favor with Germany," Darnell said, "if they spoiled your plans to align with England and France."

"Exactly."

Darnell gazed out the window at the retreating greencoats. "The police are leaving. They must have accepted the heart attack theory for the General's . . . discomfort." He regarded the Prince again. "You're safe in here. Keep your door locked. Chef Voisseron personally brings your food. But I'll be doing what I can to uncover any plot against you."

The Prince nodded. "Be careful. Every European country is on a coil spring. Lives are snuffed out

sometimes to seal the lips of those who would pass
secrets or plans, sometimes just to create antagonism."

"Let's hope it doesn't get that far here."

The Prince stood and turned to Penny. "Thank
you. Mrs. Darnell." He took her hand again and re-
peated his hand-kissing ceremony.

The Prince's valet led them back to the door, let
them out, and locked it behind them. They walked
toward the dining car.

"Whew!" Penny said. "International intrigue. What
next?"

Darnell laughed. "Have you ever been kissed by a
Prince before?"

"I wasn't kissed this time. It was an air kiss. An
inch away."

He hooked his arm in hers as they walked and
looked sidelong at her. "You sound rather disap-
pointed."

Penny took a seat at their breakfast table, joining
Madame Morgana, Agatha Miller, and courier Donald Brand, who was solicitously pouring coffee for
the nurse.

"I'll be back after I find Bayard," Darnell said, and
strode through the car. The train chugged out of the
Vienna station a little past nine a.m. As he walked
by, he noticed Anna Held was seated with a new
passenger. Train romances seemed to be as common
as those aboard a ship. He recalled how he had met
Penny aboard the *Titanic*, and smiled as the French
words for it—*amour de voyage*—popped into his
mind. But what of Anna Held's other admirer, Donnelli? He wondered how she could spend time with
two men in these circumstances.

As he passed their table he heard the words "and

the jewels were gone." He stumbled at that, but continued walking.

The two Turks and two Greeks sat opposite each other at the farthest table near the door. It was apparently their favorite and permanent post for the trip, away from the others. After the Prince's comments, Darnell saw them not merely as drinking, loud-talking men, but with possibly deeper purposes than would appear. He wondered if one could be a Pasha. The older Turk, perhaps?

He noticed a young man, who seemed intent on keeping to himself, at a small table across from the Turks and Greeks. What secret, he thought, does that one hold?

Darnell found Bayard leaving the General's compartment. "How is he?" he asked. "Did he survive the police inquiries?"

Bayard leaned against the wall. "Better than I did. I was worried the matter of poison would come up, and I certainly wasn't going to mention it. A heart attack. That's what they wrote in their book."

"What did Miss Miller say?"

"I kept her away from it. Mata Hari—I mean Miss Zelle—talked of the heavy drinking . . . She's staying with him." He raised his eyebrows. "The cheese, protected by the mouse?"

"We shall see." Darnell made a gesture of sipping from a cup. "Breakfast, Pierre? You could use some nourishment."

Arturo Donatello, alias Anton Donnelli, watched Anna Held leave for breakfast with her new escort, apparently the Philippe she had spoken of at dinner the night before. He was aware the man had boarded at Vienna and that she called him "a friend." Sounding less than forthright, it bothered him. But they'd be occupied for a while. This was his best chance to do what he must.

He tried their connecting door, but found the deadbolt had been thrown and could not be opened. He stepped into the corridor and, with a metal picklock, let himself into Anna Held's compartment and locked the door. He unlocked the connecting door. That would be his quick escape route if needed, and she would not remember whether she had locked it or not that morning.

He proceeded quickly, opening her valises and gently sifting the contents, being careful to put each item back exactly as found. Long years of experience had given him a precision that would deceive any owner. They would never suspect their cases had been rifled—until it was too late.

He found the jewels in a small metal case in the bottom of her second valise, and opened the case in a few seconds. A sparkling necklace, earrings, bracelets of gold and diamonds, a string of pearls, and more rested inside.

Donatello hesitated for some seconds with his dilemma. Should he take them now and risk her wanting them before the trip was over? Or take a chance on getting to them before Budapest the next day? The decision took half a minute. He scooped up all of them and dropped them into his pocket. From his other pocket he produced a quantity of paste jewelry he had brought for this specific purpose, placed them in the metal case, relocked the case, replaced it, and relocked the valises. With that weight, if she didn't open the case, it would seem untouched.

He locked the connecting door between their compartments, stepped to her hall door, and looked out. No one there. He stepped out into the corridor, his picklock in hand, and locked her door. A moment later he was inside his own compartment relocking the connecting door. Suddenly a wave of unexpected remorse swept through his body as he thought of her soft lips and the touch of her body the day before. He had seduced women before, and stolen from them, but his feelings were different this time. He poured a stiff shot of brandy, tossed it off, then poured another.

In the dining car, Anna Held had glanced up at Professor Darnell as he passed by, and continued her story. Philippe Cuvier had expressed his shock and asked her to tell him more.

"The theft was almost eight years ago, but I'll never forget it. It was right after one of Flo's big shows." She smiled, remembering. "I was never in Flo's *Ziegfeld Follies*, but starred in his other musicals. The jewelry, you see, it was my own, not stage jewels. One piece was worth thousands, the lot as much as a hundred thousand." She grimaced. "I was heartbroken."

Cuvier pursed his lips for a whistle, but instead merely said, "What a loss."

"It was on a train, just like this one. Can you imagine?"

"Train thieves are common. Soon they'll be boarding trains and holding up passengers as they did in the Old West in America. I heard of one such incident last month."

"My God! I won't show another piece of jewelry this trip. Anything I have will stay locked up." Noticing his appraisal of her, the slight narrowing of his eyes, she added, "And that isn't much."

Cuvier said, "You're leaving the train with me at Bucharest? My business takes me there. The weather will be lovely."

Anna Held looked into Cuvier's gray eyes. Somehow she saw less compassion in them than she had found in Paris. Perhaps Paris has that effect on everyone, she thought, and it wears off. Anton's voice drifted across her mind, with a remembrance of the feel of his hands on her, the night before.

She sighed. "I . . . I don't know, Philippe. They say the Bosporus is beautiful this time of year. I may go on by ship to Constantinople." She shook her head, and forced a smile. "But this is too deep a subject, and English is too cold a language. Speak to me *à la Parisienne.* I miss speaking French."

At the breakfast table, Penny was amused at the fresh gossip about the General's condition and the source of his ailment, knowing what Darnell had told her. With some difficulty, she joined the conversation, holding back that knowledge, as well as what she had learned from the Prince. But others made up for her reticence.

Madame Morgana left nothing to the imagination as to her views. "These are dark hours. It all builds up to something desperate. I feel it."

"As a *voyante,* Madame," Brand asked, "are your psychic powers constant—even at breakfast? I thought a séance was necessary."

She shook her head, her long earrings jangling, clinking. "No. Only to reach the departed soul. I may have a flash of recognition, a revelation, at any time. And my verses come."

"Your quatrains?" Agatha Miller smiled.

"Yes. Even now something presses on my consciousness."

Agatha said, "Would you like a headache powder?"

"You can scoff," the Madame retorted. "This is a train of death."

"I was only joking."

Brand looked at Agatha Miller, eyes twinkling, and said, "And I thought it was a train of dreams."

"You have read Sigmund Freud's study?" The Madame scowled. "On this train, dreams could be more than they seem."

Penny laughed. "We hear different versions of what this particular train, the Express, is all about. The Security Chief for the Orient Express told my husband that it's the secret agent line."

Brand nodded. "I can believe that. In fact, I must believe all of the attributes ascribed to this train—death, romance, and, no doubt, secret agents, too."

Darnell and Bayard walked to the table and took seats. The waiter approached, poured coffee, and took their food orders.

"Did I hear the words 'death and romance'?" Darnell asked. "A potent combination."

"Potent, and dangerous," the Madame said. "Now it comes to me, my quatrain." She spoke the words sonorously,

> *The wheels of destiny turn round and round.*
> *Their revolutions make a lustful sound.*
> *The syncopation may cause some to sigh,*
> *yet before dawn comes, one more may die."*

Agatha Miller shuddered visibly. "I'm glad you said may instead of will. We have a chance, then."

Darnell said, "That isn't a self-fulfilling prophecy. *Man* makes events happen—not poetry."

Penny rested her hand on his arm. "Tell that to Shakespeare, John. Couldn't one of his sonnets—or one of Elizabeth Browning's—make an event happen? Like a romantic response? That melts someone's heart?"

He smiled. "In affairs of the heart, yes. I admit that. But I spoke of death." He gazed out at the passing landscape as the train rumbled on, and his last word seemed to hang in the air like a cloud over the table.

They finished their meals in virtual silence. Afterward, the Madame stood, saying she was going to the ladies' salon.

Donald Brand took Agatha back to the caboose, where he had discovered it was possible to be completely alone on the platform and watch the track disappear behind them. "You have to see that," he said.

Bayard left to attend to his duties.

Penny took Darnell's arm and said, "Now let's put your poetry theory to the test—the romantic theory." As they strolled to their compartment, she heard the hypnotic sound of the wheels of the train and wondered how it was affecting her husband. Inside their room, Darnell took her in his arms and dispelled her doubt. Wheels were turning round and round.

Chapter Ten

Mata Hari took the General's hands in both of hers. "You are calmer, now, *mein General.*" She pronounced the *G* as an *H* to find if her German accent could make him smile. "Do you *sprechen ze deutsch?*"

He rewarded her with a grin. "Don't seek employment as a German interpreter. Stay with your dancing."

She laughed. "I'm glad you're feeling better. You must watch your heart."

"Too much to drink in one night. Or maybe, too much French wine, not enough good German beer."

Her face was serious now. "But you know about the . . . poison. You were lucky to be too sick to drink much of it."

"I heard."

"What have you done to someone on this train, Klaus—or what do you *plan* to do? You're still in danger, you know."

"You know I cannot tell you what my charge is. That will be revealed in due time. But, as things are . . ."

"War rumors? Entanglements? Conspiracies?"

He nodded. "You know the world today. Everyone listening for the word, watching for the one event that starts it all. But even the walls sprout ears and eyes."

"Then we must talk of something else."

"Shall we talk of love?"

"That wonderful word again . . ." She smiled gently as he took her in his arms. "Yes, we'll talk of that. But you must remember your heart, General Klaus. And also remember mine."

Darnell looked at Bayard across the small table by the window in the train manager's compartment. "You ask, what next, Pierre? Do you mean, what will *happen* next—or what do we *do* next?"

Bayard chewed away the last bit of thumbnail on his right thumb and frowned. "Both. I just want this train to get to Bucharest with my passengers—how do the Americans say it—'in one piece'?"

"I'm as much concerned about you, my friend, as your passengers. Are you all right?"

Bayard let out a deep breath. "I employ you to search out a ghost, and now all this. Is one thing caused by the other?"

"It's not technically a ghost, you know."

"What?"

"As I understand it, the Duchess, the woman whose apparition has been seen, is still alive somewhere. You said she still has liaisons with the Baron, the armaments king. It can't be her ghost."

"An apparition, then, a phantom. It's a memory of what happened that night, a memory wandering on this train. And always finding its way to compartment seven."

Darnell smiled. "I wouldn't talk of such things to your Board. Not just yet, anyway. I think there's more to learn about that. And the connection among the apparition, the Major's death, and the General's situation? None that can be seen."

"So—what do we do next?"

"If you're prepared for it—the Turks. And the Greeks."

"Ha! *Declassé!* You scrape the bottom."

"Yes, the bottom of the barrel as they say in America. They also say there, 'to get to the bottom of things.' Who knows what we'll find there." He stood. "Come. Let's see if your train is a modern Trojan horse."

Bayard led the way to the compartments with common doors shared by the two Turks and two Greeks, a few doors from his own room in car two. He rapped on the door. "It's M'sieur Bayard—may we talk? *S'il vous plaît?*"

There was a rustling inside, as of a straightening of the room, and muffled words. Shortly, the door opened a crack and the Turk known as Gaspar showed part of his face through the opening. His black hair was rumpled, his shirt out.

Darnell caught the odor of strong spirits, possibly a mideast drink, from two feet away. The man's drooping mustache was moist, apparently with drink.

"What do you want?"

"To talk. The Professor and I have some questions."

Gaspar's eyes shifted toward Darnell. "Questions?"

Bayard's tone firmed. "Please open the door, now."

Gaspar stepped aside, and flung the door wide. As they entered, he made a slight bow and seemed close to losing his balance.

Darnell felt the man would make a good character in a motion picture. Three other men stared at Bayard and himself from their places at the window seat. A bottle stood on the small table between them, and four glasses.

"You would like, perhaps, something to drink?" Gaspar asked, looking from one to the other.

"No—we will not be long."

Darnell said, "I understand the four of you take this train often."

Gaspar nodded. "We like trains."

"You go back and forth, it seems, on the Orient Express."

"There is no better way to travel."

"Your purposes? The purpose of this trip?" He studied the others by the window as Gaspar obviously searched for an answer. The other Turk, Nasim, gray-haired, had a faintly distinguished look about him. Could he be a Pasha? A former Vizier? The two swarthy Greeks opposite him at the table looked less promising from the standpoint of intrigue, yet they were here.

At length, Gaspar answered, clearing his gravelly throat conspicuously. "We travel. We sell. We make a living. Goods from Turkey, for credits in Paris." He pronounced it *Paree*, with a flourish. "We enjoy ourselves on this train. It is a crime?"

"Not at all, Pasha." Darnell watched his face.

Gaspar jerked, and the other Turk at the table spilled his drink. "How—I—what do you mean?"

"Ovar Pasha, correct?" He looked at the gray-haired companion at the window. "And Heggar Pasha?" He bowed slightly at the other man, in imitation of the Turk's earlier gesture.

"Sir," the Turk said, as his companion rose. "We must talk of this—I mean, you must *not* talk of it."

The white-haired Turk stepped over to Darnell and spoke in a rumbling, volcanic voice. "Professor. Yes, Professor Darnell. We have heard of you. But not as, what you seem now, acting as a detective. More, as a psychic."

"I explore the world of the psychic. I rebut it. I don't participate in it. Yet it leads me into strange corners."

"Dark corners, yes. Where danger can lurk."

Darnell laughed, then said, "Excuse me, Pasha, but that is a bit dramatic."

"These are dramatic times. So . . . you know our identities." The Turk scowled. "Then all I could say may have crossed your mind."

Darnell nodded. "And perhaps my answer has crossed yours."

The Pasha's eyes narrowed. "In the years ahead, millions may die if certain things become known. It is dangerous to interfere in events when you do not know the attitudes of all the parties."

"But it's more dangerous to precipitate events, than to observe them."

Heggar Pasha said, "So, we understand each other, then?"

"Entirely." Darnell turned to Bayard. "Pierre? I think we can go now." He turned and opened the door. Bayard stepped through it as Darnell turned back to the Pasha and said, "Enjoy your trip."

Gaspar—Ovar Pasha—stared at Darnell with cold eyes. "We hope yours is successful—for you, and for your wife."

Heggar Pasha's face was unsmiling.

Ovar Pasha slammed the door behind Darnell and Bayard, who stood now in the hall regarding each other. Bayard's eyes were wide. "How did you know?"

Darnell brushed away the question. His lips twisted into a sardonic smile. "Your Trojan horse did offer some surprises."

But as they walked back to the manager's compartment, his smile faded. The Pasha's sly reference to
his wife carried with it a veiled warning. For the first
time, he regretted bringing Penny on the trip. The
Turk gave him new reason now for making sure
Penny was never alone. "Dangerous to interfere,"
Heggar Pasha had said. Darnell patted his .38 special
in his pocket. That Turkish sword, he thought grimly,
can cut both ways.

"It's a strange sensation," Agatha Miller said to
Donald Brand, "to see the landscape and tracks fade
away from you in the distance." Her gaze was fixed
on the optical illusion of the train tracks seeming to
come together a half-mile behind them.

Donald Brand looked at Agatha Miller's profile
and decided this was his best chance to talk with her
about his feelings.

He had persuaded Albert, the conductor, to let
them sit on the back platform of the caboose, and
even provide them with two chairs there. Albert
scratched his head. "My passengers usually like the
comfortable salon cars. But—all right. Just remember—if you fall off, you risk my neck."

"Ours, too," Brand laughed. "We'll be careful." He
handed him some coins. "Now, bring us some champagne, and you'll have done your duty."

They sat sipping their drinks and admiring the private view. The nurse bundled herself in a large,
bulky sweater, which she pulled closely around her.
Brand turned up his coat collar. The air was invigor-
atingly cool, with a touch of moisture from recent
and recurring rain. The noise of the whirring, clatter-
ing wheels on the iron was, in its way, restful. Occasional flecks of soot drifted down through the air.

In her relaxed reverie, Agatha Miller felt a sense

of adventure she had never known before, and relished the feeling. Yet even in this environment her thoughts ran toward her writing, and her yearning to plan stories, to pass on her feelings of adventure and mystery to others.

"Donald . . . tell me about the Major. About his death."

The young man hesitated. "I . . . I know the facts aren't clear. But he must have had some reason for his suicide. He never talked to me much. I knew him only slightly at headquarters, and on this one trip."

"Did he seem depressed at all?"

Brand shook his head. "You could never tell what he was thinking. At least I couldn't. He was abrupt, not very humorous, a little pompous, very old guard."

"And you . . . are you the opposite—casual, funny, down to earth and avant garde?"

He laughed. "I hope some of those. I'm a bit too serious, I'm afraid. It could be the nature of my calling."

"As a spy?"

"A courier."

She frowned. "And what is in your mysterious briefcase?" She nodded at the brown case. "You never let it out of your sight."

"It was the Major's responsibility. I don't know what's in it—honestly. I just had to take it on. All I know is I must get it to our people in Bucharest as soon as we arrive. It's up to them to open it."

"Could the case—I mean, its contents—have something to do with the Major's death?"

"The case wasn't taken from our compartment."

She frowned. "Oh." She was silent for a moment. She pointed toward a farmhouse they were passing. "Can you imagine the lives of people who live

there—Austrians of course—but farmers, simple
folk? Simple lives. How would they feel on this train,
with this luxury, yet with this danger?"

Brand looked at her. "No different than we do.
Awed, intrigued, a little afraid. Wanting to make
sense of it all, along with everything happening in
the outside world, too."

"Someday," she said, in a determined tone, "I'll
capture it all in my stories—my feelings, I mean. I'll
travel, and write. That'll be my life, Donald."

"I was hoping—well, now that we know each
other . . ."

Agatha Miller focused on Donald Brand with eyebrows raised. He apparently was thinking something
that she wasn't. She should have made that clear.

"Donald . . . I should have told you this . . . I'm
betrothed. Our wedding is scheduled already, in December. By the end of the year, I'll be a married
woman."

Brand's eyes widened in surprise. "Married? I . . .
I didn't know." He looked down, then drained his
champagne flute. "We'd better get back."

"I'm sorry if you misunderstood."

He picked up the champagne bottle. "There's some
left. Let's at least finish it with a toast."

She nodded and he divided the remainder between
their two glasses. "Here's to you, then," he said, not
a little quavering in his voice, "and to the memories
of our trip on the Express."

"Cheer up, Donald," Agatha said. "We're still
friends."

Brand frowned at the word "friends." It had an
air of dismissal about it. They clinked glasses, and
tipped them back. They walked silently back to the
first-class car. When he left her at her door, he turned

away quickly. He felt she could have been very important to him—if the world had been different.

Elizabeth Arnaud shook her husband's shoulder. "Wake up."

He opened one eye and regarded her blearily through it, then opened the other.

"We've missed breakfast. We have to get ready for lunch."

He yawned. *"Oui.* I suppose food must be eaten, even on a honeymoon."

"Yes, my dear." Her forehead creased. "But there's something else. The woman in the blood-soaked nightgown—I saw her again."

He sat up. "The same as the first time?"

"Yes, exactly. The sound of her woke me. I saw her again, I blinked, and she disappeared from the corner at once. So I didn't bother you." She shuddered. "The Professor questioned whether it was a nightmare the first time. I don't know anymore what is reality and what is a nightmare."

He took her in his arms. "You're trembling." He held her closely for a moment, then looked into her eyes. "What we told the Manager—you understand that must not change."

"I know, and I've been honest. My sensations have been genuine, but I can't explain them."

He frowned. "Whatever it is that's happening, I am here with you. You're safe. So, we talk of other things. You must, how do you say, get it off of your mind, yes?"

"But the Professor—he knows about these things. Can't we talk with him?"

Tony Arnaud hesitated. "If you're afraid . . ."

"I'm not afraid. I just don't understand myself."

"Then it's best that we do nothing. If anything happens again, you will wake me?"

"Yes."

"We'll get dressed now, and have a nice lunch." He looked out the window. "We reach Budapest soon. Let's see what we can of it, to compare it to my Paris."

"The mysterious Budapest, yes." Elizabeth threw off the covers and her mood, as she stepped out of the bed. "Let's enjoy our honeymoon. Maybe we can find a Gypsy shawl for our baby." In a sing-song voice, she murmured, "Bye, baby, bunting . . . that's an old English nursery rhyme, Tony. Daddy goes a-hunting, for a bunting. Let's get one, to wrap our baby in."

Chapter Eleven

Luncheon on the Orient Express, Darnell decided, as he glanced about the dining room, no longer reflected the innocent gaiety of travel of the first night. At the far-end table sat the Turks and Greeks, exuding their usual laughter and noise, yet when Heggar Pasha, who was facing him, caught his eye, the Pasha's gaze became cold and steely. Their raucous behavior, Darnell now knew, was an act, an attempt at deception.

Anton Donnelli, who sat, without a companion, opposite Darnell and Penny at their table, occasionally glanced over his shoulder at the table where Anna Held and her new companion sat, and Donnelli frowned as the woman offered him a sympathetic smile. Agatha Miller and Donald Brand were at a table for two. Madame Morgana sat at a window table writing on a notepad, presumably, Darnell thought, composing more prophetic quatrains. The mysterious young man sat, as usual, alone at a small table.

Also at the Darnells' table sat the focus of much attention among the passengers—General Klaus Eberhardt—in his first visit to the dining car since his experience of the night before. Mata Hari sat next to him, attentively, and Darnell reminded himself to refer to her as Miss Zelle.

"You're feeling better, General?" Penny asked.

He revealed his gold fillings in a broad smile. "It is hard to kill a German, especially a General. Our stomachs are brought up on good German beer and sauerkraut. There is nothing more lethal than that."

"Did something happen last night?" Donnelli asked.

Darnell realized Donnelli had not been seen at breakfast or throughout the morning. Was he peeved that Anna Held had a new suitor? He answered Donnelli for the General. "A stomach upset—mixing drinks and heavy food."

Mata Hari nodded. "The Orient Express is a place where indulgences are part of the fare."

"We pay to be pampered," Donnelli said, unsmiling.

Chef Voisseron and Pierre Bayard came from the direction of the royal car of the Prince and stopped at their table. Bayard addressed all those at the table. "The Prince sends his regards. He would like to host a dinner party tonight."

Darnell asked, "Where? In his car?"

"No. They feel confined. He and his secretary will come out here. We'll put tables together for one special long table for everyone from first class, and some others. A party table."

"How wonderful!" Mata Hari exclaimed. "We'll all have a chance to dine with a Prince."

"Chef Voisseron will direct the service for the table himself," Bayard said, "and I'll select our best wines."

Penny beamed. "How exciting!"

But Darnell frowned.

"We must tell the others now," the Chef said, bowing, and he and Bayard moved on to the next table.

Penny turned to her husband. "John, does this remind you of the dinner party Sunday night on the *Titanic*?"

"The *Titanic*?" General Eberhardt broke in. "There is a story in that name."

Darnell gave Penny a warning glance and answered. "We were among the survivors, but we don't like to speak of it."

"Of course." The General eyed Darnell. "You've been through an ordeal as bad as war. But war will be a worldwide ordeal—the strong will survive, not merely women and children."

Donnelli cleared his throat. "I've heard of general strikes being planned against the war. Maybe there's hope of peace."

General Eberhardt shook his head. "They may try, but there are many things that can bring war—the rebuilding of the military, the smoldering hatreds, the treaties, the pent-up energy. War will come."

Penny said, "But not before our dinner tonight, General. Not before our party. Let us enjoy that." She linked her arm with Darnell's and smiled across the table at the others.

Anton Donnelli smiled in return, then glanced over his shoulder at the woman at the table across the way. When he turned back again, a deep frown had replaced his smile.

After lunch, Darnell found the train Manager, alone, in the men's salon, checking supplies of after-dinner liqueurs, mixed nuts, and snacks. "This party is dangerous, Pierre. How can we protect the Prince if he's accessible to everyone on the train? And how will you handle his food? He was sensitive to that."

Bayard raised a hand. "I argued all of that with him, John. I think his companion, Zizi, asked him for the party. She's bored. And they're both young, so naturally they like parties. It's the *joie de vivre*."

"You didn't answer—what will you do about the food? The Prince wanted a food taster. Will you taste his food for him?"

"No. But I'll watch its preparation, along with the chef, and have Voisseron serve it to him." Bayard examined a fingernail, then bit off a portion of it. "I . . . I think the Prince has another motive. He wants to see who is here, who might be an adversary."

"And if he identifies such a person—then what?"

"I don't know."

"At least, we'll need to have his two men in the dining car, on guard—armed, not eating, just watching."

"I'll arrange that with the Prince," Bayard said.

Darnell studied the Manager. "You seem calm enough with all this going on."

"Calm?" Bayard shook his head. "I'm at my wit's end. Yet . . . there is one positive thing about it."

"The royal party, correct?" Darnell's lips twisted into a wry smile. "Passengers will pass the word they dined with a Prince on the Orient Express."

Bayard looked down. "I admit it will be good for business."

"It will, if all goes well. If not . . ."

Bayard cringed. "If not—I won't be here to worry."

"Entertainment," Penny said to Darnell.

"What?" Darnell looked up from the train timetable and brushed back long strands of hair from his forehead. "Entertain who?"

"Entertain the Prince, darling! Don't you realize we have three entertainers aboard? A dancer from the shows of Paris, a singer from the stage of New York, and a fortune-teller."

"They may not want to entertain."

"I could ask."

"You'd act as the entertainment committee?"

"We could use some entertainment."

"Well, you'll have to ask Bayard, and clear it with him."

Penny smiled. "He'll love it, I'm sure."

Darnell checked his watch. "I'll be asking Bayard to take me up to the engine for a while. That could take an hour."

"The engine? Why?"

"Security. I want to inspect it, talk to the Engineer, see how things are controlled. You can talk with Bayard when he returns." He paused. "I have to tell you one thing, if you're going to talk with the women. The dancer, Margaret Zelle, is, well, more than she seems. Her stage name is Mata Hari."

"She's Mata Hari? That's wonderful!"

"But wait—you can't use her name. She insists on keeping her privacy. If she agrees to perform and asks about it, tell her you'll refer to her as Margaret Zelle."

Penny frowned. "How long have you known about her, John—and why didn't you tell me sooner?"

"I've known since this morning, since the General's seizure."

"Thank you for the late news." Her voice was flat.

Darnell touched her hand. "Penny, apart from the General, no one knows except M'sieur Bayard and Agatha Miller, simply because they were both there this morning."

"All right." She grinned. "I'll keep your little secret."

"One more thing. Remember what I said—be careful. Talk with the women in the ladies' salon, where it's public. Don't forget Major Coulton's death and the attack on the General . . ."

She sniffed. "A suicide and a heart attack, M'sieur Bayard says."

"Maybe, maybe not." Darnell frowned, visualizing Ovar Pasha's face. "There are other things. Just promise you won't be alone with anyone—except the women."

Penny's laughter filled the room. "You're jealous. You don't want me alone with men!"

"I want you alive."

Learning from conductor Albert that Bayard was reviewing dinner plans with the chef, Darnell walked to the kitchen and found them in heated conversation about the pâté.

"Sorry to interrupt you, Pierre, but can you give me a few minutes?"

After they stepped into the corridor, away from the others, Darnell said, "I'm still concerned about security for tonight. I'd like to inspect the engine, and ride in it for a bit."

Bayard laughed. "Some of our royalty have driven an engine. Is that what you want?"

Darnell smiled. "No. Just an inspection."

Bayard glanced at his watch. "We'll reach the next stop in a few minutes, and the run from there to Budapest is forty-three minutes. You can ride in the engine for that stretch."

"Perfect."

At the next stop, they pulled on heavier coats and walked up the platform to the engine. Bayard introduced Darnell to the engineer, Able Duncan, and the fireman, Sandy Porter. "Our English crew," he said. "The Professor just wants to observe your procedures," he said. "He'll ride up here with you to Budapest." Bayard left Darnell in the cab and headed back to the dining car.

The bell clanged in response to Duncan's pull, and the train chugged out of the station. Darnell watched the engineer and fireman busily going about their work. Huge clouds of steam were released down about the wheels, as the train moved, at first slowly, then gathered momentum as the long main rods connected to the wheels moved forward, backward, faster and faster. Smoke and steam belched into the air above the engine and trailed back over the train in a quickly disappearing steam cloud and a longer dark smoke cloud. Duncan hit the whistle when a crossing appeared in view, and touched it again as they neared it.

"People who live along the line know my whistle," Duncan said. "They know every engineer's—they're all a bit different. Mine is a long one, followed by just a touch on it."

"You used the bell leaving the station, I noticed." Darnell kept his balance holding a steel post next to the Engineer. He watched the landscape speed by and felt the wind in his face.

"Entering and leaving stations," Duncan said. "Clang, clang, you know. Folks hear that, as a warning. But also, they just like the sound. Like I do."

"I can see you enjoy your work, Mr. Duncan."

"Call me Able. It's from the Bible, but spelled different. My old dad was a preacher."

Darnell raised his eyebrows. "Mine also. In America, when I was a boy."

Duncan offered a gap-toothed smile. "A train engineer's job is a sort of religious thing—it gets into your spirit as well as your blood. I couldn't do anythin' else." He paused. "It's a musical thing, too."

"Really? How?"

"Listen to the engine, the wheels—it's like a waltz. Chug, two, three, four, chug, two, three, four. Music to *my* ears, anyway. Every engine has its own ways. This one's like a livin' thing—she breathes, and she groans with her aches and pains. Sometimes I think she even talks to me."

Porter winked at Darnell. "Able gets a bit balmy about her. I think he loves this old hunk of metal." He opened the firebox door again and stoked it with several shovels of coal. "She's hungry, today. Course, old Able here, he's pouring out a lot of steam right now . . . Givin' the Professor a show, Able?"

Duncan nodded. "Not yet, but let's open her up. It's a long stretch here, no crossings."

Darnell watched as Porter tossed coal rhythmically into the firebox—scoop, turn, toss, scoop, turn, toss—sweat beads forming on his forehead. This one man made the train go.

Duncan pulled his cap on tighter and pressed down with his right foot on the footplate, increasing the speed. His face took on the look, Darnell thought, of a conductor leading an orchestra, or a painter examining his subject. It was a creative look, and one of intense pleasure.

Duncan said, in a voice loud enough to be heard over the engine's din, "Tell us what you want to know, sir, we're glad to answer. We don't get many visitors in the cab."

Darnell raised his voice also. "Have you ever had big problems with the engine or the train—any danger to passengers?"

Duncan removed his cap, scratched his head, and replaced the cap, pulling the brim down tight. "Must keep it snug," he said, "or the wind'll take it. Problems? Well, two years ago, I had a spot of bother.

Three mugs tried to jump down on my tender car from a bluff, but we were going too fast, and I opened up the steam. They fell off, and got bloody well skinned up."

Able looked at Sandy Porter. "About all the trouble I've had. But Sandy, you were here in '01, weren't you?"

The fireman looked up from his shoveling. "You mean when the train jumped the rails? Not half! The bleedin' engine ran right into the restaurant at Frankfurt. At lunchtime, too. No one hurt, though, not even Pascal, the engineer."

"M'sieur Bayard mentioned royalty driving the train . . ."

"Hah! Yes, sir," Duncan said. "I won't say which King—but one of them would come up here and take over the footplate. He loved it, didn't scare. I tell you, them were some wild rides."

Porter said, "But one Prince was so afraid of bein' shot, he locked hisself in the water closet for three hours."

Darnell smiled. "Sitting on the throne?"

Duncan and Porter laughed.

They fell silent as they coped with the great speed of the train. Porter continued his steady stoking of the firebox. Duncan's gaze was fixed unwaveringly on the track ahead. "Comin' into Budapest soon," he announced.

Darnell felt the train slowing down, the engine moving less in its side-to-side dance to the wheel music. Now it slowed more dramatically, and it soon crept into the station, making the slow waltz-time sound Duncan had described. The engineer touched the whistle, one long, one short. He pulled another strap and the bell began to clang, announcing their arrival. At the platform, the engine eased to a slow, grinding halt, and a cloud of steam was released from the cylinders at the ground level.

"We're here, sir," Duncan said. "An' it's been a pleasure, indeed."

Darnell shook hands with the two men, Duncan and Porter pulling off their heavy gloves to take his hand. "Thank you, Able, and Sandy. I know we're in good hands with you two up here. Take good care of your engine."

Darnell stepped down onto the platform. Bits of ash and soot floated down, and he brushed them off his coat. He felt comfortable that no one could get onto the engine except when the train was stopped at a station. He walked down the platform toward the sleeping car.

Chapter Twelve

While Darnell was in the engine on the way to Budapest, Penny met Bayard as he left the kitchen, and explained her plans for entertainment. With his exuberant approval for the idea, she decided to talk with the three women together, feeling that if one agreed, the others, although reluctant, would be more compelled to entertain also.

She picked up Madame Morgana in the second car, stopped at Anna Held's compartment, asked her to come with them, and they walked forward to Mata Hari's compartment. The four women went on to the ladies' salon, which they found to be unoccupied.

Penny seated herself opposite the three of them. "I didn't want to be mysterious," she said, "but I felt we could talk better together, the four of us, about the dinner party tonight." She paused. "Dining with a Prince, I thought we should have some entertainment for him, something we could all enjoy."

The three women exchanged glances. Madame Morgana spoke up. "Entertainment for the Prince? I visualize jugglers, clowns."

"No, just what we have here, with us. We're so fortunate to have wonderful entertainers like the three of you on the train. I'm hoping each of you

will be willing to perform at dinner for the Prince—
and for all of the rest of us, of course."

Anna Held spoke. "I might be willing to sing, but
I would need accompaniment."

"We have our string quartet—do you have music
with you?"

"Of course. What singer travels without music?"

"Then you'll sing?"

Anna Held glanced at the others, who were studying her. "If all of us agree, I will do it. One song."

"And you, Margaret. Will you dance?"

"I have one costume with me. Why I brought it, I
don't know. I'll do one dance. A dance fit for a Prince."

"And Madame?" Penny looked at the psychic, feeling she had won her battle.

"What would you have me do—tell the Prince's
fortune? I cannot do that. Any private fortune I tell
remains so. I make no personal predictions or disclo-
sures in public." She glanced at Anna Held, and
Penny felt the two had a secret between them.

"All right," Penny urged. "Then, your quatrains.
Give us one or two of those. They're impersonal
enough."

The Madame's dark eyes returned to Penny's gaze
with a somber stare. "All right, I will do it. But do
not expect to find strawberry fields in my verses. The
fields I see are red, but not with berries."

"Say whatever you feel. I'm sure we'll be enter-
tained, and impressed. Especially the Prince."

She nodded. "To impress a Prince—I will join in."

"Wonderful. You'll have the afternoon to prepare.
I'll tell the quartet you'll talk to them about your
music. Now, let's have some tea."

Bryan Stark sat staring out the window. He had
thieve's remorse, and worried about what could be

happening in London. Would de Havilland return early—as he sometimes did? Would the plans be missed? He realized now he had acted out of emotion, not logic, a hatred for the man who had been unjust to him.

The thought of prison—a place he had never seen or experienced—also flicked across his mind. It would be a dark, dank place, he imagined, with rats scurrying across a wet, moldy floor. He shivered.

The knock on the door startled him, and he jumped up awkwardly, spilling his wine. Quickly he mopped it up with a handkerchief, which he stowed with the wineglass in a drawer, and answered the door just as a second knock came. He opened it to face General Eberhardt.

"General—come in." He stood aside as the officer strode through the doorway.

When Stark closed the door, the General said, "Ten minutes is all you have. Then I must get back. Let us see those plans."

Stark nodded, swept up now in his mixed feelings of wanting to show the plans, to sell them, and his worries about being caught, and about prison. He could feel his heart racing, and he tried to take a deep breath to calm down. He went to his case and took out a secondary, locked leather folder and placed it on the table. As the General watched, he unlocked it and removed one of the more than a dozen sheets in the folder, and unfolded it onto the table.

"This is only one of many views of the craft, an overview sheet. But you can see the design features. Are you familiar with aircraft?"

The General shook his head. But his eyes glistened as he bent over the table and studied the details of the drawings.

"This has interesting possibilities, very definite possibilities." He straightened up. "I've seen all I need. But these would have to be shown to our experts. They would have to see them in Berlin. You can go there?"

Stark swallowed hard. Berlin. This was getting out of hand. "I-I will think on that." Going to Berlin—Stark realized the dangers of that. It could be a one-way trip.

The General broke in on his thoughts. "Do not think too long, Stark. You mentioned Budapest. We are not far away."

Stark refolded the plans and slipped them into the leather pouch. "I will let you know. Yes, thank you."

The General sniffed. "You must go to Berlin if you are interested."

"I understand. Well . . ."

"*Guten tag*, then." Eberhardt turned abruptly on his heel and let himself out of the room.

Bryan Stark sank onto a chair. He felt his forehead and found it moist with perspiration, and blotted it with his sleeve. He retrieved his glass, poured it half-full from a bottle in the cabinet, and drained it. Now he had a new worry—the General had seen the plans. Were they safe now? He went to the door and put on the night bolt. He would have to stay in his room.

Stark's mind raced ahead. He could get off at Budapest, see the officials there, take the next train back, and replace the plans before de Havilland returned.

After walking the women back to their compartments and dropping them off one by one, Penny went on to the second car, where she found the leader of the quartet and told him of the plans. As she returned to her compartment, one of the Turks passed her in the second-class passageway.

"Mrs. Darnell," he said with his deep accent, nodding as they passed inches from each other in the narrow corridor. She could smell the heavy scent of whiskey or wine on his breath, as he turned and faced her to pass. Penny's nose wrinkled at the even heavier scent of perfumed oil, which did not cover up the man's strong body odor.

She wondered, would this man and his friends be invited to sit at the same table with a Prince?

"You are well? You enjoy your honeymoon?" His silky words were spoken heavily, and did nothing to make her feel he was simply being courteous.

She managed to say, "Yes," but felt his words held more significance than a casual inquiry.

As she walked on, she realized the man's tone suggested a sense of something beyond or beneath the words. She shuddered, but shrugged it off. It's nothing, she thought. It must be the effect of John's warnings. She shook her head and smiled. Next, she thought, I'll be suspecting the conductor!

The train was slowing now, as it reached Budapest. When the conductor opened the door, she stepped down and scanned the station for Darnell. She saw him coming toward her from the direction of the engine, and a lump came into her throat, inexplicably— as if he'd been away for a long while. She realized how much she worried about him when he was on a case, and how, underneath it all, she feared for his safety, just as he did for hers. She waved and smiled as he waved back and quickened his step.

Chapter Thirteen

Passengers stepped down onto the platform at Budapest in a steady stream, all apparently filled with anticipation at seeing the fabled city a thousand miles east of Paris.

Elizabeth Arnaud held her husband's arm tightly as they worked their way through the crowd. Residents typically came to the station, Bayard had told them, either to admire the magnificent train as it stopped on its way to Bucharest, or to sell wares and souvenirs to its passengers. Tony and Elizabeth Arnaud headed through the station to find the stalls of local merchants on the streets outside the station. "Something for the baby," Elizabeth said. "A warm shawl, a soft blanket."

Tony Arnaud nodded, but could not bring himself yet to join in her enthusiasm. There was an unreality about it all—marrying fast into a wealthy family, the honeymoon, now a child.

At first, he had been overwhelmed with astonishment at the prospect of becoming a father, but now the reality and responsibility of it were pressing down on him. He did not want to live on his wife's allowance or trust funds, whatever there were. And how could he support them with his meager sales of paintings?

He took a deep breath of the spring air. At least they had a free trip, because of the apparition. The truth about that, he knew, must never come out—until the trip was over. But it was beginning to bother him.

Anna Held and Philippe Cuvier strolled along the platform. She dropped his arm as Anton Donnelli approached them from the other direction. He nodded at them and she smiled.

"You know him well?" Cuvier asked. "There is . . . something in the way you exchange glances."

"I . . . met him on the train. We dined together the first few meals—until you arrived."

Cuvier fell silent. "It is not the same with us as in Paris, is it?"

Anna looked up at him. "Paris is special. There is something in the air there."

"Bucharest has an air, too. An air of romance. Will you leave the train, spend the week there with me? We can recapture those days, those feelings we had walking in the rain in Paris, drifting down the Seine in the boats. Those candlelit dinners."

She avoided his eyes. "I hope it may return—but other things have changed."

"Donnelli?" He thumbed behind him in the direction the man had taken.

"I can't talk of these things, Philippe. Let's just enjoy our trip, the party tonight, the time we have until we reach Bucharest." She took his arm again. "Let us give fate a chance in this. Our stars may have plans for us we do not comprehend."

"You've been talking with that psychic."

Anna Held did not answer him. Madame Morgana

walked toward them, pencil busy on a pad she carried. She looked up from her writing and smiled at Anna as they passed each other.

"Modern Nostradamus!" Cuvier sniffed. "Let her predict the financial markets, as I do. No crystal ball can do that."

Agatha Miller gestured at the briefcase in Brand's other hand. "Don't you feel odd carrying that at a station stop like this for just a half hour?"

Brand fell into step with her. "It's a bit awkward, but it's my duty. The rule is, 'Don't let it out of your sight or hands.' And with the Major gone, I had to take that role on."

"A big role for you."

He smiled. "I usually just arrange hotel reservations, ship bags, that sort of thing. I'm not a spy."

"You'll deliver it in Bucharest?"

"Right. Then I'm free. We could see the sights there."

"Donald . . ."

"All right. I give up. No more."

She looked away. "Anyway, I have to write down the notes I've taken for my stories."

"Why do you like mysteries?"

"The field is opening up for women. Conan Doyle hasn't written a new Sherlock Holmes story for ten years. I think women can put a new face on the mystery novel."

"A woman's face."

"Yes. A woman's angle and sensitivity, too, if you like." She paused. "Some women have started already. Baroness Orczy wrote *The Scarlet Pimpernel*. Then, *The Old Man in the Corner* and *Lady Molly of Scotland Yard*." Her jaw was set firm. "If she can do that, I can do it, too."

"I'm sure you can."

She mused for a moment. "Poisons," she said. "Would you say they are a woman's way of committing murder?"

Brand said darkly, "Perhaps the Major could tell you something about that, if he were here."

"Or . . ." she went on, "could it be a deception someone would use deviously to create the impression of a woman's method?"

He laughed. "I can see you're thinking like a mystery author, Agatha. You're way ahead of me. Plots within plots."

Only one or two alert passengers of the Express noticed the young man leaving the train with his coat collar turned up. He carried a suitcase in each hand. Bryan Stark had spent the last minutes before the train reached Budapest considering his plight. He was a thief now. Worse, he found himself under the cold eye of a German general who could now try to obtain the aircraft plans from him without any cost other than the slashing of a young man's neck.

Stark's throat tightened, thinking of the desperate fate he had almost created for himself. Could he get back to London before de Havilland returned? If he took the next train, perhaps.

Bryan Stark hurried to the ticket window.

Chapter Fourteen

After the train pulled out of Budapest, passengers took to their compartments for privacy or to the salons for conversation. Chef Voisseron worked feverishly with his staff in the kitchen preparing the courses for the night's special dinner, and occasionally came out into the dining room to observe progress there.

Pierre Bayard and the waiters moved tables together in the dining room into one long table, arranged chairs, and laid out the best china and silver on the white lace tablecloth. Bayard's first seating choice was easy—placing the Prince at the head of the table and the Turks and Greeks at its foot. He sensed the cultures would not mix. He set out the other place cards after much thought as to the composition of the table. Then he devoted careful attention to the stationing of waiters and musicians. The day, he knew, would go on like this until the hour arrived.

In the ladies' salon, Mata Hari and Anna Held rehearsed their entertainments with the string quartet. Madame Morgana watched and gave an audience reaction.

"The space is so limited," Mata Hari complained as she finished her dance rehearsal. "I usually have a full orchestra and an entire stage."

"Pretend you're in the Prince's bedroom." Anna Held smiled.

"Oh, God!" The dancer collapsed in laughter on the couch. "Now—now it's your turn."

Anna stepped to the front of the room and struck a pose. She sang a Broadway show song in English in her delicate, accented voice. At the end, the Madame and Mata Hari applauded. "Everyone will love it," the Madame said.

During the afternoon, the Turkish Pashas sat across from each other at the window table in the Turks' compartment, drinking and talking. "It's our best chance, maybe our only chance," Ovar said, for the second time.

Heggar Pasha shook his head. "I do not like it. At a table with twenty pairs of eyes watching. You may as well send a note, 'Come to dinner to die.'"

"Heggar, listen. If he reaches Bucharest alive, *you* will get such an invitation yourself. And you know who will send it."

Heggar shook his head. "I have invested much time in negotiations with both sides. If we show our hand now, we could lose both sides. They want what you want—they've paid us enough to indicate that. You know it. But they want a bit of subtlety—*savoir-faire*, the French say."

"But they want results," Ovar said. "Not subtleties."

"It will not happen at the table. Do you understand?"

"We are of equal rank. Only the Committee can settle it."

"But they're in Constantinople. And I am senior here."

Ovar Pasha stood. "I must bathe. I must be clean and smell good when I sit at the table with a Prince."

Heggar said, "Let one thing be understood. If anyone is to do it, I will."

Ovar smiled. "I see. You want the glory. Yes, now I understand."

Zizi Lambrino stroked Prince Carol's thick brown hair. "We will have a good time, my Prince, yes?"

The Prince nodded. "You like parties, my sweet. I give you one. It's little enough. I can't give you my name."

The woman moved closer to him, lay down next to him, and pressed her lips to his cheek. He turned his head and found her lips with his own. He kissed her passionately, then broke away. "Damnable crown! Sometimes I think I'd give it up for you."

"My Prince, you don't need to do that. We marry in secret."

"But I want the world to know."

"I would be your wife. The important thing."

He scowled. "And you would still have to act as my secretary. Act. Like an actress."

"Don't distress yourself. If you want to marry me in secret, and I have to pretend to be your secretary, I will do it. We could have the ceremony in Rome or Paris. There are places, people I know."

Prince Carol turned his head toward the window. The landscape sped by in front of his eyes, but he saw none of it. He sighed. "Our party begins soon." He put on a smile. "I wish they knew they entertain not just me, but my bride-to-be."

By eight p.m., Bayard and his staff finished their work of organizing the dining room for the dinner party. The long table was set for twenty, although several, such as Bayard and the Prince's two aides, would have to catch meals in off moments.

Bayard smiled in satisfaction at the result. Three wineglasses at each chair, crystal, china, silver, napkins folded in the shape of seagulls, candles spaced in several spots for lighting when the performances began. He hoped the Prince would be impressed and tell others in his court about the elegance of the party that Pierre Bayard presented on the Orient Express.

At one end of the room, space was provided for the string quartet, the performances by the dancer and singer, and readings by the psychic. As he thought of Madame Morgana, Bayard frowned, hoping the psychic would not dampen the party with depressing predictions. Yet, world conditions could not be avoided by ignoring them.

Chef Voisseron stood at his elbow. "We are satisfied?"

Bayard glanced at him nervously. He truly would be satisfied only when the party was successfully completed. He knew he'd worry throughout the evening. No need to let the staff know his insecurity, however. He nodded at the chef. "Yes. And I know you will surpass yourself with your presentations."

"A dinner fit for a Prince. I'll return to my kitchen now."

Bayard nodded and stepped back against the wall and breathed a deep sigh. He folded his hands behind him in a deliberate effort to avoid biting his nails.

Penny Darnell and the three performers entered the dining room a few minutes later and walked forward to preview the area set aside for them. The quartet was tuning instruments and arranging music on metal stands.

The violinist leader of the group bowed as the women approached. *"Bonsoir."*

"Good evening. Is everything ready?" Penny admired their shiny instruments—two violins, a cello, and the bass. "You've rehearsed with Margaret and Anna?"

He nodded. "Yes. We will play incidental music during the meal. Then the three performances will be before the dessert course, *n'est-ce pas?"*

Penny spoke for the others. "After the main meal, Anna Held will sing first. Then the Madame will give readings. There'll be a short break while Margaret returns to her compartment to change into her dance costume, then she will conclude it with her dance."

"Excellent." He beamed. "It is our great pleasure to play."

At the opposite end of the car, with a broad smile, Bayard greeted other passengers as they entered through the first-class coach door.

Chapter Fifteen

The hubbub in the dining car grew as passengers entered, admired the table settings, and chatted with the others as they prepared to be seated.

Penny found her place card next to the seat marked for Zizi, and Darnell's card next to hers. "Here we are, John." She motioned to him on the other side of the table. "Come around."

The men wore dinner jackets and black ties, the women their finest evening gowns. Shuffling about, checking place cards, and being seated took a few minutes.

Darnell observed the others as they found their places. He could see that Pierre Bayard had given careful thought in laying place cards to recognize the relationships passengers had shown or formed so far on the trip. The head of the table, nearest the performers, was reserved for the Prince, and on his right, his secretary Zizi Lambrino.

On the left of the Prince's chair sat Madame Morgana, Anton Donnelli, Anna Held, Philippe Cuvier, then Tony Arnaud and his bride Elizabeth. The next seat was reserved for Bayard, who said to Darnell he'd actually be on his feet most of the time managing table service.

On Darnell's right were Agatha Miller and Donald Brand, and next to them Margaret Zelle—Mata Hari to some—with General Eberhardt. The Turks and Greeks were positioned at the far end of the table. The Turks, looking to Darnell unusually clean, crisp, and well dressed, were seated last.

The string quartet struck up a lively air, not the classical pieces played at the other meals, but a song popular in the Paris cafés and music halls, setting a party mood.

Penny said, "This is so exciting, John."

"Are you going to be the mistress of ceremonies?"

She shook her head. "My part is done. I arranged with M'sieur Bayard to introduce Anna for her song, then the Madame, and Margaret as the last, with her dance."

Chef Voisseron began to open several bottles of white wine, sampling each by a small sip from the small silver sommelier cup strung about his neck, then pouring wine for the passengers.

Darnell watched Bayard head back toward the Prince's private car, knowing he would bring the Prince and his guest out quickly now for a royal entrance, since all were seated.

In a second fluted glass, Chef Voisseron poured champagne, telling each passenger, "To salute the Prince when he arrives." He filled glasses for the Prince and Zizi also, and stood waiting for their arrival.

Bayard entered the room leading the Prince and Zizi to the table. He bowed and gestured toward the two seats for them. Waiters attended Zizi's chair as she sat. The Prince remained standing.

"He's gorgeous," Penny whispered to Darnell. "Look at that uniform." The Prince's dark blue uniform, ornate with gold braid and epaulets, was enhanced by a wide, royal red ribbon reaching diagonally across his chest from his left shoulder to his right hip. A sword hung at his right side in an ornate scabbard.

The Prince lifted his champagne glass. "I toast you all, my fellow passengers on the Orient Express, and thank you for this opportunity to dine with you." He took his seat, touched glasses with Zizi, looked into her eyes, and sipped from his glass. Applause broke out, and the Prince nodded and smiled at the assemblage.

Prince Carol nodded at Penny. "I heard you have managed some entertainment."

"Yes. Just to your left in that area in front of the quartet. It will begin before the dessert course."

The Prince laughed. "I'm sure the performances will be dessert in themselves."

Penny turned to Zizi. "Your gown is lovely," she said. "It looks like spun gold."

"Thank you, yes, it does have touches of gold thread. I bought it in Paris. The Prince travels to Paris several times a year in his private car. We go with him—his valet, an aide, and I—as his secretary, of course."

"I must have means to communicate as I travel," the Prince said. "To write my father, to arrange appointments. Zizi is invaluable."

He smiled at Zizi, who lowered her eyes for a moment, then raised them to look into his in a frank gaze.

Across the table, Anna Held seemed to be making the best of a difficult situation, with a suitor on each side of her. Philippe Cuvier, Darnell thought, apparently was dedicated to trying to dominate the conversation with Anna, while Donnelli seemed oddly quiet, almost disturbed.

"Tell me more about your Broadway career," Philippe said.

Anna sighed. "It spanned almost eighteen years. I must go back once more. I left because Flo was, well, with someone else. But my audience—they expect a proper good-bye." She mused. "In the best days, I had my own private railroad car, a grand piano and complete band."

"I read you used milk for your complexion."

Anna nodded. "It was for the publicity. Flo arranged to have forty gallons of milk delivered to our hotel suite in New Jersey. He released news to the press I took milk baths." She lapsed into the accent of her early career. " 'It is zee milk bath zat preserves zee creamy complexion.' That's what I was told to say." She laughed. "But I starred in many great shows, like *Miss Innocence, Mademoiselle Napoleon, Higgledy-Piggledy.*"

"You were the star of all of them?"

"Of course."

Anna looked sidelong at Donnelli, who stared at his plate and tapped it absently with a fork, his mind apparently elsewhere. She turned away from Philippe toward Anton, and spoke in a low voice. "How are you tonight, Anton?"

He did not look up at her. "Pleased to know I'm here at all. I . . . I'm confused."

She rested a hand on his. "Do not be. All will be well."

He raised his head to look at her and saw glaring at him, from beyond, the steely gray eyes of Philippe Cuvier.

The Prince's young, mellow voice broke into the tableau as he addressed Madame Morgana. "Tell us—tell Zizi and me—of your prophecies, Madame. What lies ahead?"

She glanced from one to the other of the Prince and Zizi. "Freud has said, 'The light of reason is very dim—and always threatening to flicker out.' I will read my own words later, after Anna sings. I hope you will not disapprove."

"It does not seem a Princely prerogative, Madame, predicting the future. More likely, *controlling* the future."

"Either we control *it,* or it controls *us,*" the Madame said. "The world will learn this soon."

The Prince asked, "On a more personal note, Madame, would you say I shall obtain my heart's desire?"

"I believe, Prince Carol, you have it well within your grasp." The Madame smiled at Zizi. "Often, we merely have to reach out and embrace our desires."

General conversation waned as waiters served clear turtle soup, followed soon by a salad of aspic and cold asparagus spears, and the diners remarked upon the food.

Talk resumed between courses, and soon waiters brought the fish course of dover sole almondine. The passengers settled into a pattern of busying themselves with their food amid a buzz of conversation.

Donald Brand's gaze moved back and forth between his attention to his food and the face of Agatha Miller next to him. "Are you making mental notes, Agatha?"

"Of course. I may never have this opportunity to dine with a Prince again. It could make a wonderful scene."

Next to them, General Eberhardt whispered to Mata Hari. "I don't want to share your charms with them. Later, you must dance for me alone."

"Tonight. After the dinner." Her eyes twinkled as she whispered, "I give you . . . the encore."

Chef Voisseron walked his long circuit around the table. He poured a Bordeaux red wine, and while it was being sampled, the chateaubriand was brought to the table and carved to order. Fresh vegetables accompanied it, and a small green salad followed that. Afterward, plates were cleared and demitasses served.

Darnell divided his time between his food and observing and listening to the others around the table. He particularly kept his eye on the Prince, and any who approached him.

Conversation appeared to be ordinary enough. The Turks and Greeks seemed to be holding their own private dinner at the far end of the table, not joining others in any general talk, and drinking more heavily than the others.

At ten o'clock, Pierre Bayard stood and tapped a spoon musically on his water glass. "Time," he announced, "for entertainment."

All at the table applauded.

"First," he continued, "we have Anna Held, who will sing for us. Miss Held is more than a chanteuse, she's a New York City Broadway star, and we are pleased she will perform for us."

Applause greeted her when she rose and walked past the Prince to the front and opposite side of the car. She pulled down the short sleeves of her gown to bare her shoulders. Chairs moved as her audience turned toward the performance area.

Penny whispered in Darnell's ear, "Look. She's barefoot."

Anna Held curtsied and said, "What I wear is similar to my stage costume." She wiggled her shoulders. "Bare shoulders." She held up a foot. "Bare feet." She laughed. "It all began with my debut and my songs at the Wintergarden in Berlin. I starred in a musical called *Die Kleine Schricke*—'The Little Teaser'—and I'll sing a song from that, my trademark song."

She nodded at the violinist, and the musical introduction began. Anna Held sang in her delicate, lightly accented, lilting voice, "Won't you come and play with me . . . As I have a nice little way wiz me . . ."

She swished back and forth across the area, kicking up her feet, rolling her coquettish eyes, making provocative gestures and movements. She finished the song on a high note, lifted her skirts in a flourish, and ran back to her chair, laughing, the audience applauding as she took her seat.

The Prince raised his wineglass to her. "Marvelous, marvelous, Miss Held. Thank you." Zizi echoed his sentiments, and others added their own phrases around the table.

Bayard stood again. "Now, some special words, some predictions of her own, from Madame Morgana, who has a gift—a special gift, shall we say—of insight into the future. Madame?" He held out a hand toward her in invitation to come forward.

The Madame rose, gathered her long shawl about her, and stepped over to the performance area. She removed a ribbon from a scroll of parchment-colored paper. "I write my quatrains as they come to me—walking, dining alone, at night before I fall asleep. I write what flows into my mind."

She turned to the Prince. "Your Highness, nothing in this is intended to relate to you. These words have come to me independent of this party."

She held the scroll in front of her and read in her stage-sonorous voice, dramatically voicing the words:

"An angry patriot's pride precedes the fall
of a youthful leader who hears the call
of sirens, singing on the rocks of hate,
beckoning him onward to his fiery fate.

The streams flow red with blood of boys
who take up guns, and put aside their toys
to answer other calls for heroes brave,
while tearful mothers alternately pray and rave.

The strawberries are gone, yet fields are red,
as years stretch out, like armies of the dead.
Each King's vainglorious dream, his bold surmise,
becomes a nightmare's birth—an evil enterprise."

The audience sat silent as each person seemingly absorbed the words into his or her consciousness. The Madame returned to her seat, rolling up her scroll as she walked. When she took her seat next to the Prince, he applauded. The others at the table instantly joined in with his applause.

During the applause and talk, Margaret Zelle left the car to change into her costume.

The Prince said to the Madame, "I heard your words 'youthful leader.' You're sure . . . ?"

She nodded. "I don't know what the words mean. They just come to me. But I did not intend them, purposefully, for you."

Zizi said, "We can't say now we've had no warning of war. You've given us one."

Those at the table took refills of coffee and talked about the Madame's quatrains. The Prince asked the Madame for a copy of the stanzas, and she promised to provide it before the trip ended.

Bayard glanced at the door and saw Mata Hari—

still Margaret Zelle to most of the audience—standing just inside the door in her dance costume.

Anxious to enliven the party again, Bayard clinked on his glass with a spoon. "Now, Miss Zelle, who has just changed into her dance costume, will perform a dance for us, straight from Paris."

At his words, Mata Hari ran forward to the performance area and took a provocative position. The quartet played the first notes of the song they had agreed upon with her, and the audience watched raptly as the dancer moved gracefully, fluidly, pirouetting back and forth. She held seven veils wrapped about her, and at the conclusion of each series of positions, she dropped a veil, then danced on, and dropped another. As each veil dropped, the audience could see more of her costume underneath.

Darnell, who knew of this dance of hers, was relieved to see that she had the light costume beneath the veils, remembering talk that in Paris clubs when she dropped the last veil she was completely nude. Now, she dropped that last veil, but a filmy, low-cut short dress and skin-toned silk stockings were visible. The music swelled to a crescendo, then stopped, as she took her last turn and ran back to the door of the car, followed by loud applause. At the door, she turned, bowed, and left the car. In five minutes, she returned in her party gown, to more applause.

The Prince raised his glass to her as she seated herself and announced, "Excellent! I drink to you, fairy dancer."

Penny smiled at her and said, "You made our party complete."

Darnell took Penny's hand in his. "Thanks also to my impresario wife. Florenz Ziegfeld, at last, has competition."

Waiters brought in dessert trays under supervision

of Chef Voisseron, who walked along with them
around the table to comment on his confections. Afterward, another round of champagne was poured to
signal the end of the party, and one by one the passengers came up to the front of the table to greet the
Prince personally. In his democratic way, the Prince
shook the hands of the men, and took the hand of
each woman to give the air kiss Penny experienced,
not quite touching the backs of their hands.

Among the last to greet the Prince were the Greeks,
followed by the two Turks. As the Pashas stood in
front of the Prince, Darnell's eyes, which were upon
both of them, narrowed when he saw a movement
of one of the Pasha's hands over the Prince's glass.

The passengers all returned to their seats, and the
Prince stood once more. Darnell stood also. But as
he reached for his champagne glass, he knocked over
the Prince's glass, which spilled its contents on the
table and rolled off onto the floor.

"I'm so sorry, Your Highness," Darnell said. "Very
clumsy of me." To Bayard he said, "Another glass
of champagne for Prince Carol, Pierre. My fault,
entirely."

Bayard brought a second fluted glass, filled it, and
stepped back. The Prince raised it and announced,
"Thank you all for the extraordinary dinner and
entertainments."

The Prince took a single sip from the glass, as the
others did in imitation. He set it down and offered
his arm to Zizi, who linked hers in his. "I—and Zizi,
I'm sure—will always remember this special party."
The two walked toward his private car, followed by
his two aides.

Pierre Bayard sank into his own chair and filled
his own champagne glass to the brim. *"Voilà! C'est*

magnifique!" He swallowed half of his champagne. "Now I can relax."

The party ended at midnight and passengers returned to their compartments. Darnell took Penny to their room and said, "Lock the door. I have to talk with Bayard for a few minutes."

In General Eberhardt's compartment, Mata Hari said, "I have no music, Klaus, but I'll sing along as I give you the encore of my dance." She stepped into her own room for a minute, removed her shoes, dress, and underclothing, and positioned her seven veils. The General lay expectantly on his bed, pillows propped up behind his head.

She stepped into the room, sang softly and hummed the song, a sensual Parisian melody, and performed her dance, swirling about in abbreviated steps in the confinement of the dimly lit room.

Veils dropped at the conclusion of each series of pirouettes, until but three remained. Mata Hari danced closer and closer to the bed, dropping first one veil, then the second, and finally the last one, with soft, throaty laughter. She threw herself by his side on the bed, her body glistening.

Chapter Sixteen

The train Manager enjoyed his deserved respite and reward for a party well done, and sat at the table in the dining room sipping his champagne. When his staff came over to his table, Bayard drank a last toast to them, thanking them for their work.

Darnell returned just as Bayard's staff left. In the now-deserted dining room, they sat opposite each other at the end of the long table. Rain began to pelt the windows and thunder reverberated through the car, along with the steady sound of the wheels on the track. He heard the engineer's whistle, one long, one short, as they passed by a crossing.

"There's something you should know, Pierre," Darnell told the Manager. "We almost had a tragedy at dinner—one that would have surpassed anything that's happened so far."

Bayard looked up from his champagne. "But it was *sans pareil*, everything went perfectly. What . . . ?"

"One of the passengers dropped white powder into Prince Carol's champagne glass. I was forced to tip it over to keep the Prince from drinking it."

"I thought that was an accident. You mean . . . ?"

"I'm sure the powder dropped into it was poison."

"*Mon Dieu!* Who did it?"

"There's no proof, of course—the drink is gone, and any evidence of the contents. But I know what I saw. It was one of the Turks."

"A Turk!" Bayard gulped his drink.

"He was quite bold. To try that in the presence of so many—it was arrogant, yet it could have passed unnoticed. I suppose he felt no one could be singled out with everyone greeting the Prince at such close quarters."

"They're dangerous fanatics." Bayard scowled. "We'll have to tell the Prince."

"In the morning. His car is secure now. Let him have this night—and I'm sorry to spoil yours."

Bayard shook his head. "*Au contraire.* You *saved* the evening. The death of a Prince would have been a devastation for the Orient Express, and for me." He looked up, at the ceiling or beyond. "*Le bon Dieu!* He watches over me still."

The rain continued steadily throughout the early hours of the morning. As the train slowed and stopped at a small station, the lone conductor on duty at 1:20 A.M. ushered four women aboard and into the second-class car. The rain had wet their hair, and their light coats and damp dresses clung to their curves.

"You must be quiet," the conductor said. "If the Manager hears . . ." He made a motion across his throat with a finger, indicating a knife blade. He led them to the Turks' compartment and tapped on the door, which opened at once. "Your *putain*. They must leave the train at the 5:23 stop, I come back then. The rest of the money now."

Ovar Pasha pushed a bundle of bills into the conductor's hands. The Pasha put an arm around one of the women, a blonde, and said, "We must get you

out of those wet clothes." The door closed, and the
conductor walked to his station at the end of the car,
counting his money. For the next four hours he
checked his watch a dozen times and wiped perspiration from his forehead.

At the appointed hour, when the train slowed, the
conductor retrieved the women, who stepped out of
the room as soon as he tapped on the door. Glancing
in, he saw the four men laid out on their beds, apparently in drunken stupors, or asleep.

The conductor took the women to the train's outer
door and made sure they all left the train. Moments
later, as the train chugged out of the station again,
he went to his own compartment and added the
money to another sheaf of bills in his traveling bag.
He loosened his collar, poured a stiff shot of whiskey,
and muttered to himself, "Good money, but never
again."

Saturday morning, April 18, dawned with no respite from the incessant spring rain which slanted
against the windows in long, large drops. The rain
was accompanied by occasional lightning flashes and
the low rumble of thunder. Passengers slept late in
the comfort of their compartments, lulled by sounds
of rain and train.

Madame Morgana entered the dining room at 8:15
A.M. to find the tables arranged into their original
configuration and no one except a lone waiter present. She took a table by the window and ordered
juice and coffee. Her mind was disturbed by her own
verses that she had recited the night before. Was it
Prince Carol in the words for those quatrains that
came to her from a source she never could identify?
She recalled also her quatrain at breakfast the day

before, which warned of a possible death before dawn.

The Madame was relieved the night before that the Prince had returned to the safety of his private car after the party, but she resolved to share no more of these whispers in her mind with those on the train. She had to understand more about them herself.

She sipped coffee and thought of Anna Held, whose hand foretold of the singer's dark future. She was a woman much troubled by a decision between her two suitors, and worried about her future life. The Madame reflected also upon Major Coulton, who it seemed had taken his own life, and the General, who had found, peculiarly, his own life spared. This trip was a harbinger and microcosm of broader dangers she could see coming, and the Madame was anxious to reach her native Bucharest. She wanted to put as much distance as possible between her and the major European powers that she foresaw would be soon struggling for supremacy. A thousand miles, she felt, could make the difference between her own death and survival.

Agatha Miller entered the room and approached the Madame's table. "May I join you?"

Madame Morgana nodded. "We're the only early birds."

A waiter brought coffee and poured it for Agatha, who said, "I'll order food later."

"When Mr. Brand arrives?" the Madame asked.

A light blush crept up the nurse's neck to her cheeks. She looked down and busied herself with the coffee and cream. "I'm afraid he and I had a . . . misunderstanding."

"Really?"

"He didn't know I have my wedding date already set this year. I thought of him as like a . . . a shipboard acquaintance. He thought there could be more to our . . . friendship."

"So your paths will separate. But you will both return to London soon."

"Is that a prediction?"

Madame Morgana offered one of her infrequent smiles. "No, in this case, a mere observation. You are both English. When the world plunges into the abyss of war, you'll return to your homeland, for safety. Just as I go to mine now."

John Darnell awoke to the sound of pounding on the door of their compartment. A sense of foreboding swept over him. The Prince? Had something happened to Prince Carol? His face fell when he saw a haggard-looking Bayard standing at the door.

"Dress quickly, John. We have another death."

"My God! The Prince?"

"No. One of the Turks. Meet me at their cabin. I'll find the nurse." He hurried down the corridor, leaving Darnell standing at the open door. Darnell watched as Bayard knocked on the nurse's door several times, and, receiving no answer, marched on into the dining car. Darnell dressed quickly and woke Penny to tell her what he was going to do.

Five minutes later, Darnell reached the Turks' compartment to find Bayard and Agatha Miller already inside the room. He entered and locked the door behind him. Heggar Pasha and the two Greeks were also in the room.

Agatha Miller was examining the body of Ovar Pasha, which was sprawled on his bed. A knife hilt protruded from his chest. Bayard stood to one side, watching, with the Pasha. The two Greeks sat on the second bed, their heads in their hands.

"They said there was a lot of drinking—and other

things—going on here during the night," the nurse said to Darnell and Bayard. "The result—you see the knife."

"No poison this time?"

She shook her head. "I expected it, but, no."

Bayard growled, "The Pasha admitted they had prostitutes here. On the Orient Express! I swear, a conductor will lose his position this day." He trembled.

Darnell put a hand on the Manager's shoulder. "We have more important things to deal with than a conductor. Murder."

The Pasha, still wearing his nightclothes and a robe, spoke up. "One of the women must have done it. We all fell asleep, and the conductor let them out."

"Why would such a woman kill him?" Darnell asked.

"For the money. Unfortunately, Ovar showed a large roll of it when he paid the conductor. It is gone now."

"You searched his pockets?"

"Yes. I suspected that immediately. It has happened before—Ovar losing money this way. Never this violence."

"He lost money before, with *putain*?" Bayard demanded.

"Yes. They were different women, of course, in other towns."

"On this train?"

"Sometimes, yes."

Bayard groaned.

Darnell said, "We have things to do, Pierre. The body should be moved to the caboose as we did with the Major. Call your men."

Bayard nodded and left the room, after saying, "Stay here until I return."

Darnell examined the body. Ovar Pasha wore silk pajamas. The knife wound was directly over the heart. "Death would be almost instantaneous, Agatha?"

She nodded. "And it would take a strong hand to do it, at least a steady one. The blade went in between the ribs and, it seems, found its way directly into the heart."

"He was possibly overcome with drink at the time."

"From the looks of these empty bottles, and the whiskey odor on his body, I'd say, yes, very likely."

"So he would make no outcry?"

"Possibly not."

"Pasha," Darnell addressed the older man, "tell me the last thing you remember before you fell asleep this morning."

The Pasha rubbed his forehead and eyes. "I have a terrible headache, it is hard to remember . . . The women arrived a half hour before two a.m., we drank we, you know . . ." He looked at Agatha. "The Greeks and their women fell asleep first, then I fell asleep, or into a stupor from the drink. I think the women might have put something in our drinks. I've never fallen into a sleep that deep before, never had this kind of headache afterward."

"And when you woke?"

"It was morning, a little after eight. When I woke, I tried to rouse Ovar. I turned him over and saw the knife. I sent one of them for the Manager." He thumbed at the Greeks. "I stayed here."

Bayard returned with his two men. "We'll move him," he said to Darnell, "and I'll meet you in the dining car in a half hour." He and the other men wrapped the Turk's body in his blanket and carried the bundle out of the door.

Darnell told the Pasha, "We'll talk more later."

As they left the compartment, he said to Agatha Miller, "We may need you again."

She nodded. "I'll be in my compartment. Somehow I've lost my appetite for breakfast."

At ten a.m. Darnell sat at a table in the dining car drinking his third cup of coffee. Bayard walked in and announced, "It's done. We reach Lugoj in an hour. We'll turn out the body and invite the police aboard. I expect it won't take long. The Pasha wants to keep the body on the train, but I told him, we are not a morgue."

"The police will put it down to the prostitutes?"

"*Certainment.* Who else?"

"We must search the train now, Pierre."

"Search? For what? The passengers . . . they will be disturbed."

Darnell's voice rasped. "They're already disturbed. They know we've had a suicide or murder, and either a heart attack or an attempted murder. But now we have an unquestioned murder. The passengers will talk of nothing else when this news circulates."

"And what will you search for?"

"Poison, weapons, guns, knives."

"Why? You think there will be more violence?"

"The true meaning of these events isn't clear at all. What connects a courier, a general, and a Turk? And the report of the apparition by the Arnauds? And the attempted poisoning of the Prince? Could these all have something in common, and could they be directed at the Prince? We have to act as if they do and are. You'd be protecting the Prince by searching the train."

Bayard paced the floor back and forth next to the table. "This trip is supposed to be revelry and gour-

met meals and romance—not conspiracy and death."
He glanced at his watch. "And I must see to lunch
soon, after Lugoj. Passengers still have to eat and
drink. They expect it—I have a duty, and they paid
for it."

"Two paid the ultimate price for their drinks."
Darnell paused, staring out the window. "All right,
we'll wait until after lunch. Then I must insist on
searching. You can stay apart from it, if you don't
want to offend passengers."

Bayard scowled. "If we have to search, I'll lead it.
It's my train." He walked toward the caboose. He
examined his fingernails, but found none left to bite.

Chapter Seventeen

At Lugoj, Rumania, Bayard and Darnell turned the body of Ovar Pasha over to authorities. Although the rain had stopped, ominous dark clouds hung over the small town station.

Police boarded the train and held it up several hours interrogating the Manager, Darnell, the Turk, the Greeks, and the conductors. They finally agreed with Heggar Pasha's statement that one of the prostitutes had killed Omar Pasha. They took down descriptions of the women, and promised to search for them, but held out little hope of finding them. Heggar Pasha paid for treatment of the body and its shipment to Constantinople.

Darnell and Bayard walked forward to the men's salon and talked of next steps. Bayard said he would join Darnell in the search of the train, along with the conductor Albert, after lunch. "I want to use that time to interrogate the passengers also," Darnell said. "Many questions are unanswered."

Afterward, lunch consumed Chef Voisseron's energies, trying to improve passengers' spirits by providing liquid spirits. The champagne and wine flowed easily. Bayard stopped at each table, apologizing for delays of the train, now a day late.

He answered passengers' questions about the Turk, but gave little information. At a certain point, passengers absorbed what he told them, turned inward at their tables, and formed their own courts of justice.

"The Turk's death puts a different light on the other two happenings," Donnelli said to the others at his table. "In Italy, we would suspect the Black Hand Society is on the train."

Madame Morgana said, "In today's world, these tragedies are no surprise."

"Please don't make any more predictions, Madame," Agatha Miller said. "They seem to have a habit of coming true."

"We'll be in Bucharest tomorrow," Donald Brand said. "What else could happen in less than a day?"

As Brand spoke the words, John Darnell arrived late and sat down next to his wife. Penny took his arm in hers and said, "I ordered for you. The sole."

Darnell nodded and sipped his champagne.

"Can you tell us anything, Professor?" Donald Brand asked. "M'sieur Bayard said the Turkish man was killed by someone no longer on the train. It's all very mysterious."

The others nodded and looked expectantly at Darnell.

He said, "A woman—actually several women—boarded the train last night. I won't go into why. They left at a subsequent stop. This morning, the Turk Ovar Pasha was found dead, and the police suspect one of the women killed him."

"Now what?" Agatha asked.

"We'll talk with everyone about the events on the train. Most leave at Bucharest, just a few go on by ship from Constanta to Constantinople."

"It's been a trip I won't forget," Agatha said.

Donald Brand looked out the window and said

nothing. She glanced at him, and frowned, as if surmising what he was thinking.

The interviews began at two p.m. Bayard, Darnell, and Albert went to Heggar Pasha's compartment first.

"More questions?" The Pasha glared at them.

Argus and Demetrius, the Greeks, sat at the table by the window, watching. It seemed to Darnell they spent as much time in the Turks' compartment as in their own, next door. The connecting door between the two rooms always stood open.

"We must eliminate weapons on this train," Bayard said. "Do you have any?"

"No."

"Albert will search here, and next door. You and the others don't mind?"

"Search. We have no knives, no guns. Nothing to hide."

Albert began to rummage through the drawers, clothes, and suitcases of the two Turks.

Darnell asked the Turk, "Have you thought about the killing of Ovar Pasha by the woman—how it happened, or why she did it? She had put knockout drops in your drinks, I believe you indicated. What about Ovar's?"

"I felt drugged. Something was in my drink. But, maybe not in Ovar's. Or, perhaps he did not take enough, and woke while they were taking his money, which forced her to kill him. He could not defend himself well, in his condition."

"You've never seen the women before?"

"No."

"You and Ovar had no disagreements? Nothing involving the women, for example?"

The Pasha glared. "You are suggesting I had something to do with this?"

"I'm looking for information," Darnell said.

"I was drugged. I woke up and found him dead. That is the news I must carry back to my homeland. Bad, embarrassing news."

Bayard asked the two Greeks similar questions, but they added nothing to what was known. Albert found no weapons.

In the corridor afterward, Bayard asked Darnell, "Do you believe them?"

"They're holding something back, we can be sure of that. We'll try again, later. Madame Morgana is next door. Let's talk with her."

Madame Morgana readily gave permission for Albert to search her compartment and expressed willingness to answer questions. "Any way I can help, I will."

"Did you hear anything last night," Darnell asked, "between the hours of say, one and six a.m.?"

She shook her head. "I sleep heavily, and dream deeply. It would take much to wake me."

"You heard no one cry out?" Darnell pressed. "It was just next door."

"No, but I shudder to think a man was being killed ten feet away from me as I lay in my bed." She directed her gaze at Bayard. "This is not the Orient Express I know. A place of murders."

"One murder, madame," Bayard said.

The madame said nothing in response, but her eyes did not leave his.

Bayard smirked. "Your psychic powers desert you, madame?"

Her lips twisted into a wry smile. "Not exactly. I predict you will have a hard time explaining all of this to your Board of Directors in Paris."

Bayard cringed. "I think we've seen enough here, John. Thank you, madame. Come, Albert." He turned to the door.

Tony Arnaud draped the Gypsy shawl about his wife's head and shoulders. "*Voilà*, you are a Gypsy!"

Elizabeth laughed. "I feel like a Gypsy. A thousand miles from home. Heading for the Greek Islands."

"And . . . the baby—all is well?"

"It's too early to feel any movement. But I feel different. Just knowing." She frowned. "I wish I could tell my mother."

Tony nodded. "I feel bad. Stealing you away. Will they speak to me ever?"

"Of course. You'll be the father of their grandchild. That means a lot."

A knock came on the door.

"Who is it?" Tony looked at Elizabeth quizzically.

"The Manager, probably. They're asking questions."

In the corridor, Darnell said to Bayard, "You do the questioning of the Arnauds. I want to search the room myself."

Tony opened the door. "M'sieurs. You wish to come in?"

Bayard said. "*Si'l vous plaît*," as he, Darnell, and Albert entered. "We're sorry to disturb you, but we must search your room to be sure no one has concealed any weapons here."

Arnaud looked at Elizabeth. "All right—but weapons? We certainly have none."

Darnell said, "I'll look about if you will ask your questions." He walked to the closet and began rummaging in it.

Bayard took Tony's attention. "You are aware of

the death of the Turk—you may have known him as Gaspar."

"We heard, but we never knew him. We did know the Major."

"Yes, an unfortunate suicide . . . So, you knew nothing at all about Gaspar?"

"There are rumors that a woman killed him." He frowned, hearing Darnell snap open their suitcases, and glared at him.

Bayard caught his eye again. "We need to know whether you see any connection with these deaths and your apparition?"

Elizabeth answered. "Connection, no. But I did . . . well, experience something, whatever it was, again. On the second night."

Bayard's eyebrows went up. "The same as the first time—just as vivid, the blood . . . ?"

She looked at Tony, who gave a slight nod. "Yes. Exactly."

Tony's voice rose. "Please do not remind my wife of that. It is too disturbing, in her condition."

Across the room, his back to them, Darnell found a slim volume in a suitcase. Seeing the title, he quickly slipped it into his coat pocket. He glanced back at the others and satisfied himself that no one had seen him do it. He closed the case.

Tony, still with an edge to his voice, said, "Do you have other questions? We can tell you nothing about the Turks."

Darnell said, "I've finished my search. The room is clear."

"Then we are finished," Bayard said. *"Merci beaucoup."*

After lunch, Anna Held pleaded a headache and begged off spending the afternoon with Philippe Cuvier. In her compartment, she took her Pomeranian, Henri, in her arms and said, "We must talk, my *poupée*, you little doll. I neglect you." She stroked the dog and plunged into her dark thoughts.

Indecisions had plagued her since she left New York, and had now increased with her two suitors. Philippe offered security, but she could not forget the touch of Anton's hands.

"Who do you like, Henri?" She stared out at the dark sky, trees and meadows flashing by in a blur of greens and grays.

"Oh!" She uttered the sound involuntarily when a light tap came on the door connecting her compartment to Anton Donnelli's. "It's Anton," she whispered as she put her dog down. "Yes?"

"I have to see you. Please open the door."

Anna slipped the bolt across and opened the door. "May I come in?" He stood facing her.

She nodded, her heart beating fast, and stood aside as Anton entered. "I've missed you. You're always with—that man."

She shook her head. "A friend only. From Paris."

"You said at the dinner party, 'All will be well.' What did that mean?" He pulled her gently against him and kissed her. She could not resist. Her doubts fell away.

"Come with me when we leave the train at Bucharest?"

Breathless, Anna said, "I don't know, I am torn."

A knock on the door came unexpectedly.

To the door she said, "Just a minute," and to Anton, softly, "You must go." She locked the connecting door behind him.

The Manager, the Professor, and a conductor stood in the corridor. "We have some questions, madame," Bayard said. She nodded as they entered.

"My wife and I enjoyed your singing immensely at the party," Darnell said.

"Thank you. She was a delight to organize the show." Her smile was wry. "Like a female Ziegfeld."

Bayard said, "We must search your cabin to be sure nothing has been secreted here, and Professor Darnell has questions."

"You may search." She looked openly at Darnell. "I'll answer your questions, but there is little I can say."

"Did you know any passengers on the train previously?"

"Only Philippe Cuvier. We met in Paris."

"You've not known him long?"

"It was a few months ago, and only for a week then. Is there some . . . suspicion?"

"No. We merely explore. Do you know his field of work?"

She frowned. "Business, finance—but it is best you ask him."

"You and he—you will be leaving the train together?"

Firmly now, Anna said, "No. At the same stop, Bucharest, yes. But together, no."

Albert said, "I'm finished, M'sieur Bayard."

"Then we are also, madame." Bayard glanced at Darnell.

Darnell said, "Thank you."

Anna locked the corridor door after they left and stepped back to the connecting door. She slipped the bolt open and tapped on the door. She realized she had made her decision, and was eager to tell Anton.

Chapter Eighteen

Leaving Anna Held's compartment, Darnell checked the time. "I'll look in on Penny, Pierre. I don't like to leave her alone too long."

He stopped by their compartment and looked inside. "Not here. Let's try the ladies' salon." His step quickened.

Bayard instructed Albert to stay in the sleeping car until their return to resume their search.

They found Penny and Agatha Miller having tea in the salon. Although he had no specific reason for concern, Darnell exhaled a breath of relief to find her there in a calm, commonplace setting.

She smiled as they walked into the room. "Just in time for tea. We have a large pot."

"Give us two cups, just as it comes," Darnell said. "How are you?"

"I'm fine. Agatha and I were just playing detective, going over the cases."

Darnell sat next to Penny and took her hand in his. "So you're all right?"

Bayard sat opposite them.

Penny frowned. "Why wouldn't I be? You worry too much, John. We'll be fine." She filled two cups with tea and passed them across. "Have you found what you're looking for?"

"We're not sure what we *are* looking for," Darnell said. "But we'll know it when we see it."

Agatha said, "If you need anything I can help with . . ."

"I'm glad we *don't* need you, Agatha." Darnell smiled grimly. "It seems we only call you in for the dead, or near-dead. But, did you and Penny come up with any new theories?"

She smiled. "Only some I may use in my book. I do think all three events are connected. The poison was the same for two."

"We agree on that. The question is, how are they tied in?" He finished his tea and stood. "I'll look over the men's salon."

Bayard stood also. "Then I'll do a search in here."

"Meet me in the corridor when you're finished."

When Darnell returned from the men's salon, he found Bayard waiting. Bayard spread his hands and said, "Nothing."

Darnell nodded. "The same. Back to the sleeping car now."

At Anton Donnelli's compartment, they asked Albert to join them again and were admitted promptly to Donnelli's room. He was alone and seemed to expect them.

"Come in. I know you want to search. Go ahead."

While Albert rummaged, Donnelli answered their questions, but seemed distracted. "There's something I have to tell you, Professor. I know you're investigating things that seem, shall we say, unusual on this train."

"Go on."

"That first morning—when the Major was found dead . . ."

"Yes?"

Bayard held up a hand and interrupted. "Albert, I see you're finished. Wait in the hall, please."

The conductor bowed and left the room.

"Go on, Mr. Donnelli," Bayard said.

"Well, I saw a man enter the Major's compartment as I returned from down the hall. He didn't see me."

Darnell's eyebrows rose. "Who was it?"

"I'm not sure," Donnelli said. "The door was just closing."

Darnell pressed. "Someone else was visiting him? It wasn't the Major or his assistant, Mr. Brand?"

"That's right. Someone else. But I can't give you much of a description."

Bayard spoke up. "Keep this in confidence. As far as others are concerned, forget you told us."

Darnell asked again, "You merely saw him enter the compartment, his back, nothing more?"

"That was all I *saw*. Of course, I did *hear* something—voices, at least one loud voice. It seemed like an argument. It was brief, and through the walls. Then I heard the door open and close—by that point I was listening. After a moment it was quiet."

A loud knocking came on Donnelli's door. Annoyed, Bayard pulled the door open and glared at the intruder, Chef Voisseron.

The chef looked anxious, saying, "I must talk with you alone, M'sieur Bayard. At once."

The Manager turned to Darnell and said, "Some kitchen problem. Excuse me. I've heard enough here—you continue." He left the room and the door closed loudly behind him.

Darnell asked Donnelli, "Why are you telling us this now?"

"I'm glad the Manager left." Donnelli spoke rapidly. "I couldn't tell you what I saw before without drawing too much attention to myself. But now, I need your help."

"Come to the point."

"If you appreciate the information I gave you, then I ask that you help me."

"Tell me what it is. I'll decide."

Donnelli blotted perspiration from his forehead with a handkerchief. "I-I took something from a compartment, and now I'm desperate to return it."

"You stole something?"

"I admit it."

"And what did you steal?"

"Jewelry, from Anna Held—but I don't want the jewels! It was a big mistake, and I want to put them back. Will you help me?"

Darnell studied the man's face, his wide eyes and furrowed forehead. He could see pain in the eyes, and felt the sincerity of the man's desire, but Darnell's voice was harsh. "Tell me how you think it could be done, and why I should help a criminal in any case."

Donnelli cringed. "Yes, it was a crime. But I've thought of how to redeem myself. If you could be sure she dines at your table at dinner and doesn't return to her compartment when I go to it, I'll have time to replace them in a few minutes."

"When would you do it—as soon as we are seated at the tables?"

"Yes, I'll say I forgot something I must do. She'll be coming in to dinner with me, and after we're seated, I'll excuse myself. It will take but ten minutes."

"You could do this without my help."

"I have to be sure she won't come back to her room, that someone will keep her engaged."

"Let me see the jewels."

Donnelli lifted his suitcase up on the table, unlocked it, and produced a box. He opened it and displayed Anna Held's jewelry.

Darnell picked up each piece and examined it carefully. "Seems real enough." He paused, thinking of the various possibilities. "You're a professional train thief?"

"I have been. But I will give it up."

"And why should I help you at all?"

Donnelli's face looked anguished. "It's Anna—you know."

"So it's romance? And this flush of passion—it came after you stole her jewels?"

"I know it's hard to believe all this, but yes. I only realized it today, myself."

Darnell thought about the actress and what he'd observed of her since the train left Paris. "This new suitor—Cuvier? What about him—and how do you know she returns your feelings?"

"She told me today. She'll let him know before Bucharest."

"You could confess the theft to her, Donnelli."

He shook his head. "I'm afraid to risk that. She might never forgive me. I have to return the jewelry before she discovers it is missing. Tonight could be my last chance."

"And in the future . . . ? You'll continue to steal jewels from other unsuspecting, vulnerable women?"

"No! No more thefts."

"Do you realize these could be someone else's jewels? That you could be using them as a subterfuge to gain entrance to another compartment to steal others?"

Donnelli smiled. "You think like a thief, Professor. But you'll find that's not the case."

Darnell asked himself what Penny would say, and

knew what her answer would be. He also knew he'd tell her all about it.

"The only way I'll get involved, Donnelli, is to actually watch you put the jewelry back. That means my wife would have to engage Anna in conversation to keep her at the table. If my wife agrees to participate in this, I'll do it. Otherwise, not."

"All right, anything."

Darnell checked the time. "Now, back to that man . . ."

The door burst open and Bayard rushed to Darnell's side. "I must speak with you. Come quickly, please."

Darnell told Donnelli, "We'll have to talk later. I'll see you at dinner."

Bayard took Darnell's arm and pulled him into the corridor, closing the door behind them. The chef stood outside the door, waiting. Bayard said, "Let's go to my compartment, where we can talk in private, the three of us."

They hurried down the corridor, Bayard in the lead, Darnell and the chef following, and were quickly inside the Manager's compartment.

"Look at this note," Bayard demanded.

Darnell opened the folded single sheet of paper and took in the block-printed words at a glance: "A bomb is on this train. You must find it."

"You found this note?" Darnell looked at the chef.

The chef shook his head. "No, m'sieur, one of my men discovered it cleaning up the dining room. He found it among the dishes in the kitchen, in the bottom of a bread serving dish. We cannot tell which table it came from."

"Could one of your men have written it—as a joke?"

Bayard said, "I thought of that and asked them. They all deny it. I believe them."

Darnell said, "Then, Pierre, we must take this seriously. It's a stronger reason than ever to complete our search swiftly."

"Who do you think could have written it?"

"That's not the main concern at this moment. If there is a bomb, we have to find it, and soon. Get two more of your men to help with the search. I want them to scour the kitchen and dining room, every compartment in second class, the caboose, even the tender and engine, looking for anything odd, out of place."

"And if they find it . . . ?"

"Tell them not to disturb it, but let me know where it is. I'll deal with it. Meanwhile, I'll continue my search."

Bayard said, "I'll take care of it at once," and rushed from the compartment, followed by the chef.

Darnell watched them run down the corridor and took stock of the search. Four rooms left to be searched in the first-class sleeper—Donald Brand's, Mata Hari's, the General's, and his own.

He headed for General Eberhardt's. When the General answered his knock, Darnell found Mata Hari there with him, their connecting door open.

"I'm glad you're both here. I'll be searching your compartments if you don't mind."

The General nodded. "I hear you look for weapons. There are none here, except this." He produced a German Luger pistol from his pocket.

"You should give me that for safekeeping."

The General's voice rasped, his anger bringing out his German accent. "*Nein!* I vas almost killed. It vill be needed for my protection, and for hers." He nodded at Mata Hari.

"We'll deal with that later. I'll search now. Please unlock and open your suitcases and briefcase."

The General stiffened and seemed ready to object again, but he threw up his hands. "There are confidential documents in my case—do not read them." He pulled the suitcases and briefcase over to him and fumbled with keys.

Darnell opened drawers and looked in cupboards and every place a bomb could be concealed, in both compartments.

"Now your suitcases and briefcase."

"Do not study any documents."

"Don't be ridiculous, General. I don't read German, and I'm not interested in your papers. Open everything quickly. We have no time to lose."

The General eyed Darnell. " 'No time to lose,' you say. There seems to be too much urgency here. What are you not telling us?"

"Your cases now." Darnell's voice was unyielding.

Mata Hari nodded at Eberhardt. "Do it, Klaus. Let's be finished with this."

General Eberhardt opened his suitcase and briefcase and laid them out flat on the floor. He stepped away. "Search."

Darnell examined them speedily, but overlooked nothing. He set aside the documents and concentrated on looking for evidence of poison, weapons, or explosives. He found none. He stepped into Mata Hari's compartment and did the same with her cases.

When Darnell returned, Eberhardt stood. "So that is all?"

"Only this—it's imperative we gather any information regarding the two deaths on this train, and the attack on you. If there is anything you know you've not revealed, tell me now. Both of you may still be in danger."

"I've told you all I know."

"You have no idea who put poison in your drink? Nothing to tell at all about the Turk's murder, or Major Coulton's death? All of this is a complete mystery to you?" His eyes bored into the General's.

"Nothing. We hear the rumors, everyone does."

Mata Hari nodded in agreement.

"Now, your pistol—remember, it could be used against you if it fell into the wrong hands."

General Eberhardt stuffed the gun in his jacket pocket and snapped the pocket shut with an air of finality. He glared at Darnell. "I am a German general. I take that responsibility."

"Very well." He looked at both of them. "If anything else comes to mind, you'll let me know at once?"

"Of course."

Darnell took his leave, unsatisfied with their answers. General Eberhardt, he thought, knows more than he is telling. And Mata Hari knows everything the General does—and perhaps even more.

Chapter Nineteen

Pierre Bayard rejoined Darnell as he left the General's quarters. "My men are searching everywhere," he said. "No stone, as you say, will be left unturned."

"Don't forget your own compartment. That would be too ironic, to find a bomb under the Manager's bed."

"I'll check it when we finish with first class. What now?"

"The courier's room. Then mine, while you look through yours. If nothing turns up, we'll search the Prince's car."

"Agreed." He smiled. "It is odd—I was just thinking of my Security Chief, Vachel, in Paris. The 'little bull' would give his eye teeth to do this search, like his old days on the *Surete*."

Darnell scowled. "You can regale him with stories about it when we return. I hope you'll have nothing to tell."

Bayard rapped on Donald Brand's door, which opened shortly. "I suppose you're here to ask more questions."

"The Professor will do that. I'll search your quarters."

Darnell stepped into the courier's compartment, in

which the first death had occurred. He felt, unexplainably, that the answers were here, where it all started.

"My suitcase is unlocked," Brand said. "The other two are the Major's, and they're open also. Help yourself."

"We'll need to go through your diplomatic pouches and cases," Darnell said. He felt uneasy, and anticipated trouble, as he had encountered with General Eberhardt.

Brand stiffened. "Professor, even I haven't opened Major Coulton's briefcase. The Major's key hasn't left my wrist since I took it from his body."

"Then this will be the first time."

Brand said nothing.

"A few questions," Darnell said. "That morning—when you found the Major dead on your return from breakfast—was it your honest impression he committed suicide? Or . . ."

"I told you what I knew. I mentioned his poison pill, of course. I'm sure he had one. But whether he took it . . ."

"What do you feel?"

"Well—honestly, I don't think the Major was the type to take his own life. But that leaves murder, doesn't it?"

"Yes. Did you have any impression someone else had been in your compartment while you were at breakfast?"

He shook his head. "Nothing was disturbed. The only thing of serious value was his case, and that was still here."

Bayard stepped over to them. "I found nothing. I've searched every likely place now except the pouches and briefcase, and they're locked."

"Yes." Darnell faced the young man. "The keys please."

"I-I don't know. I have my duty."

Darnell's dark blue eyes were steely. "Donald, I must tell you something confidential—someone has warned there may be a bomb aboard this train. We've searched almost everywhere else, and, frankly, I think this room is the most likely place for it."

"A bomb?" The young man's eyes widened.

"Yes. Now, the keys."

Brand hesitated for a moment, but heaving a deep sigh, removed a key from his wrist and two others from a pocket. "This one is for the Major's case. These two are for the mail pouches."

Darnell bent over the pouches, which seemed to be filled with papers. He opened them one at a time and sifted through the contents. Envelopes and sheafs of reports, nothing more.

He hefted the briefcase carefully in his hands and looked at Brand. "It's heavier than I would expect. You've never seen inside it?"

"No. I'm not sure the Major did, either. A courier just *delivers* papers, Professor. We don't read them."

Darnell placed the case on the table, fitted the key into one lock, then into the second, and lifted the lid. He removed papers which lay atop a false bottom. He clicked it open.

Brand gasped, "My God!"

Four sticks of dynamite lay attached to the bottom of the case, wired in a complicated manner to a clocklike device. The numbers on the face of the clock read from 1 to 12, and a single hour hand pointed to 12. A second hand had begun a first sweep around the face of the clock.

"It's a time bomb, Pierre! Twelve minutes to zero.

It must have become activated when the case top was opened."

"*Mon Dieu!* The next stop is half an hour away."

Darnell gripped Bayard's arm. "We have to stop this train immediately."

"What will you do?"

"I'll get this . . . damned thing as far away from the train as possible. Tell your engineer to stop the train, now. Hurry."

Bayard ran from the compartment. Darnell visualized the Manager pulling a cord to notify the engineer, but sensed that Bayard would probably run forward to the engine and notify Duncan himself.

Brand stammered, "Can—can I do anything?"

"I've removed all the papers. Take them." Darnell closed the case carefully. "You won't see this briefcase again." He strode from the compartment and down the corridor, the case under his arm. He found Albert at his station at the end of the car.

"Albert—I'll be leaving the train. The Manager is stopping it, and you can help me with the door."

The conductor's eyes widened. "This train never stops between stations."

"It will this time. Come."

As they walked to the door and Albert opened it, they heard the train whistle sound, then the rush of steam released by the engine as the wheels churned more slowly in engineer Duncan's waltz time. The whole frame of the train seemed to shudder as it slowly ground to a halt. That took over a minute— just over ten minutes left, Darnell guessed.

Darnell stepped down to the ground and scanned the landscape. Two farmhouses a half-kilometer away.

He ruled out that side of the train. Too dangerous

to go that route. He knew the land on the other side was all fields, rolling hills, and woods.

To get there, Darnell saw it would save time to go around the rear of the train. He took long strides toward the caboose, watching his steps carefully, aware that he could not afford to fall or drop the case. The bomb might explode on impact.

Darnell reached the rear of the train, crossed the tracks, and walked purposefully across the fields toward distant trees, through thick brush and tall weeds still wet from the rain. He calculated his remaining nine minutes—four minutes over, three back, and two for the train to leave the area and get clear of the explosion. He imagined the minutes clicking off, one by one, as he walked. Dismal thoughts came to him—what if the clock did not really cover twelve minutes, or was not accurate?

When he reached the edge of the hills, he glanced back at the train. He realized his time was rapidly disappearing. He had walked at least four minutes, only half a kilometer, but it would have to be enough. He carefully laid the briefcase on the ground, turned, and ran back toward the train. Halfway there he slipped and fell among the slippery foliage, and hit his head on a fallen tree. Stunned, he rose unsteadily and ran faster.

When he reached the caboose, he saw Albert standing on the back platform.

Albert called out, "Get on here, sir, it will save time."

As Darnell swung aboard the caboose, Albert stepped inside and pulled a signal cord three times. "I told them that would mean you're back on board," he said. "M'sieur Bayard is at the engine."

The train chugged forward, slowly. "Can't this damn train go any faster?" Darnell asked, not really expecting an answer. But it gradually picked up speed, and in a minute was moving rapidly down the tracks, away from the site of the briefcase and the bomb it contained.

They stood together on the platform, both staring in the direction of the spot where Darnell had placed the briefcase, although they could not see the case. Darnell heard Duncan's typical long whistle and short blast, and wondered whether the train was approaching a crossing, or if it was Duncan's salute to their leaving the site of danger.

At that moment the explosion came, a huge blast, even at the now considerable distance, and Darnell and Albert stared at the smoke rising in the distance two miles back. Darnell realized he was holding his breath, and let it out with a deep exhalation.

Albert said, *"Mon Dieu!"* and sank back into a chair.

"Yes. Thank God. It's over."

But even as Darnell said the words, he knew questions remained. The source of the bomb had to be investigated. The immediate danger might be over, yes, but the mysteries remained: Who planted the bomb? Did that person kill the Major? Was it all related to the attack on the General and the murder of the Pasha?

He shook his head to clear the cobwebs and pushed hair back from his forehead. These questions could wait until he found Penny to tell her he was all right—and until he had a stiff jolt of scotch.

Chapter Twenty

John Darnell ran forward and met Penny in the corridor as she ran back from the ladies' salon. He swept her into his arms.

"John! You're safe," Penny exclaimed. "Thank God!"

He held her tight and kissed her. "Let's go to our room."

They walked, his arm around her, the few steps to their compartment. Inside, Penny clung to him. "You could have been killed, you fool. Walking around with a bomb."

"Bayard told you?"

"Yes, on his way back from the engine. We all saw you walking across the fields, then running back, but didn't know what it was all about. Then he told us you found a bomb in the Major's case."

Darnell nodded, released her, and stepped to the cupboard. He filled a water glass half-full of scotch and took a gulp, then a second.

"Whew! I think I'm having a reaction to the whole thing." He sank down on the bed.

Penny sat next to him and put her arms around him. "Just relax, John. It's all right now, isn't it?"

"Yes. As far as that danger, the bomb—it's over."

He thought of the same words he'd said to Albert a few minutes earlier, and his own reservations as to that conclusion.

"We can celebrate tonight at dinner."

"Penny . . . I don't want to worry you, but things that are happening bother me. The dangers are increasing. You have to be careful."

She laughed. "You tell *me* to be careful after hiking across the meadow with a time bomb."

"We don't know who put that bomb in the Major's briefcase. But whoever did it murdered the Major—it wasn't a suicide. That makes two murders, Coulton and the Turk, plus the attempt on the General's life. But the bomb could have killed you, and dozens of others." He pulled her close. "My duty is to you, now, to keep you safe until we reach Bucharest."

"John, I know you're not going to abandon this case. You're going to solve these mysteries."

"Your safety is more important than anything else."

"I can take care of myself. Besides, why would anyone want to harm me?"

Darnell paused, realizing Penny had actually touched on the exact source of his concern. "Whoever it is might try to get at me through you." His face was grim. "But you're right, I have to find out who . . ."

Someone rapped on their door. Darnell stared at the door, not moving. "Maybe they'll go away." Another rap came.

He sighed. "I'll answer it."

Bayard stood there and held out his hand. "Congratulations—and *merci*! The passengers all thank you. And the Prince told me he wants to talk with you personally, when you can."

"I need some time now with my wife, Pierre. I'll see him at the dinner hour."

Bayard nodded, closed the door, and left them to themselves. "Until dinner."

Darnell finished his drink and took Penny into his arms. He knew he was still recovering from the ordeal. "Some honeymoon, darling. Can you believe all this?"

She smiled. "And we thought the train just had a ghost."

They lay together, peaceful now, oblivious to the landscape speeding by outside the train, and lulled by the sound of the wheels and the motion of the train. The early evening dusk found them still entwined in each other's arms, asleep.

The feeling of excitement at dinner that night rivaled that of the previous night's party, although tension was in the air. The buzz of conversation included the word "bomb" in almost every exchange, one remarking on it, another expressing concern, a third agreeing.

John and Penny went first straight to the Prince's private car, where he and Zizi were preparing to dine. The chef was bustling about their table.

"Professor, and Mrs. Darnell, please come in," the Prince said. He stepped forward to Darnell and threw his arms about him. "You have saved us, my friend. I will never forget it." He took Penny's hand for his air kiss.

The Prince smiled at both of them and said, "Come here."

He walked back to the table, opened a silver case, and removed a polished wooden box. "This is for you, my gift to you, Professor." He smiled at Penny. "A gift to present to whomever you wish."

He held out the box to Darnell, who opened it with Penny looking on. Inside it, they saw a gold pendant set with three diamonds, on an ornate gold chain.

Penny gasped, and looked up at the Prince and Zizi.

Zizi's eyes twinkled as she said, "You will love it."

Darnell looked at the Prince, who said, "Take it out, it's yours."

Darnell picked up the pendant gingerly, unsnapped the hook at the back, and stood behind Penny, draping it about her neck. He stepped back in front of her and smiled. "You look very royal in that."

The Prince put his hands on their shoulders and said, "Now go—show the rest of the passengers your new decoration."

Zizi hugged Penny. "It looks like it belongs on you. The gold goes with your dress."

Penny smiled. "It's so beautiful, it'd go with anything."

After profuse thanks to the Prince, they left his coach and walked arm in arm back to the dining room.

"I still can't believe it," Penny said, as she looked down and touched the pendant.

The richness of the piece caused Darnell to think of Anton Donnelli, and the criminal's pledge of giving up his career as a jewel thief. Would the sight of it weaken the thief's resolve, and remind Donnelli what he would be missing in his reformed life?

Agatha Miller stared at Donald Brand. "That bomb was in the briefcase all this time! And you were carrying it with you every minute, inches away."

He nodded. "Inches away from you, too. I can't believe it. When I think of that, I shiver."

"But there's nothing to worry about now. We can enjoy the dinner—perhaps one last one."

Brand looked at her. "The last one on the train, yes. But we're both leaving at Bucharest. We could have dinner there."

"I can't do that, Donald. You know why."

"I had to try one more time, now that it's all ending."

Agatha broke away from his gaze. "Oh, look. Here they are. And would you look at what Penny's wearing!"

All heads turned in the direction of the Darnells as they approached their table and sat opposite Brand and Miss Miller.

"What a gorgeous pendant!" Agatha said to Penny.

Penny smiled. "A gift from the Prince. But John earned it, not I." She looked at Darnell. "The Prince is very generous."

Darnell did not answer. He was watching Anton Donnelli, who stared at the pendant.

Anna Held, next to Donnelli, also gazed openly at it, as did the other passengers. "*Magnifique!*" she said.

"Darling?" Penny touched Darnell's arm. "Did you hear me?"

"Oh, yes, very generous, indeed."

Madame Morgana, who sat next to Penny, said, "It seems something good has come from all this."

Darnell smiled wryly. "You say it reluctantly, Madame."

"I yield to good news slowly. Like your removal of the bomb, for instance."

"You are very good at finding clouds in a blue sky."

"I wonder, where did that bomb come from, who

put it in the case, what will they—whoever they are—do now?"

Darnell stared into the psychic's dark eyes. "Those are exactly my concerns. But you should be able to answer that last question yourself. You see the future."

"I see the broad map of the future. I picture the terrible war that will consume us all, the legions who will fall by the thousands, millions. Yet, the individual soldiers—they're faceless, like portraits without features." She shook her head. "But I mustn't spoil the party. Let us celebrate. Could you order us some champagne, Professor?"

Darnell nodded, but he was watching Donnelli walk toward the door. He turned to Penny. "I must go to our compartment for a few minutes."

Darnell looked back as he walked away and noticed that Anna Held's gaze traveled along with Donnelli. He was pleased to see her turn to speak with Penny, and that he had not needed to confide his mission to his wife. The pendant was engaging them.

He stopped to speak to Chef Voisseron. "Champagne?"

The chef smiled broadly. "Of course, m'sieur. The Manager has ordered it for all tables—it is just coming."

Darnell stepped through the doors into the first-class sleeping car and found Donnelli standing several doors down in the corridor. When he reached Donnelli, he asked, "Now what?"

"We'll go in through my room. The connecting door is open." He unlocked his door, stepped in, and closed the door after Darnell followed him. "I'll get the jewels now." He went to his suitcase, unlocked it, and took out a large scarf. He unrolled it to reveal several sparkling pieces of jewelry.

"Let's move fast," Darnell said. "She mustn't become anxious."

"I know." In the next room, Donnelli opened the suitcase, retrieved the box with the paste jewelry, replaced the genuine jewels in it, pocketed the imitations, and locked the box in the suitcase. In five minutes they were back in his room. "Done." He locked the imitations in his case. "Thank God! And you."

Darnell shook the man's hand. "All right, it's done. You return first. I'll follow in a bit."

They left the compartment, Darnell going to his own to allow a minute or two to pass, Donnelli heading forward to the dining car. After waiting briefly, Darnell also returned to the dining car. When he arrived, he found an air of jubilance.

Applause broke out, and the quartet struck up a lively tune, just as he stepped through the door.

"He arrives," Bayard called out, above the noise. "Let us all drink to him."

Darnell was amused at the musical sound of many champagne glasses clinking together as he walked to his table.

"Welcome to your party, Darling," Penny said. "It was the Manager's idea." She handed him a glass of champagne. "Drink up."

He touched his glass to hers. "I'll drink to us. And to a peaceful trip home." He gestured at the pendant. "Nice little trinket you have there."

As Penny laughed, Donnelli caught Darnell's eye and shook his head. Darnell interpreted the movement: *No*, Donnelli was saying to him, *I'm not interested in stealing the pendant—I'm a new man.*

Donnelli turned to Anna Held, and the two gazed

into each other's eyes with what Darnell perceived to be a fresh and untainted look. He hoped it was an honest one, that Donnelli would justify his confidence in him. This little story, he realized, was one he would enjoy telling to Penny on their trip home.

Chapter Twenty-One

That night, following the dinner, which for most, detraining at Bucharest, was a farewell event, the spring storm resumed in force outside the train.

In the engine cabin, the secondary engineer, Malcolm Kelly, wiped the moisture from his goggles and complained to Beauvais, the stoker. "This bloody rain buggers."

Beauvais grunted. "Nothing on the line this time of night. Just watch for cows."

Kelly's eyes never left the track as he answered, "Our cow catcher will take care of 'em."

"Duncan asleep?" Beauvais tossed coal into the firebox with his shovel in his rhythmic style—scoop, stoke, scoop.

"Not half. Sleepin' it off, most likely."

"Likes his rye." The stoker's mouth turned up at the corners.

Kelly nodded. "After the bomb scare—I don't blame 'im. He took it well. Solid as a rock when he's up here, he is, wouldn't touch a drop working. Just likes his evenin' nip."

He touched the whistle two times, then a long third one.

"You love that whistle," Beauvais said. He stopped to wipe his brow. "You're going to miss it."

"It's music, lad. Music to the ears."

The rhythmic sound of the wheels in their accelerated waltz time seemed to confirm his opinion. Malcolm Kelly stared ahead into the dark night and driving rain and thought of all the years he'd spent in the noisy, rattling, shaking hunk of metal he called his second home, and the fact that this would be his last trip before retiring and returning to England.

Kelly wiped the raindrops from his goggles. But his vision was still blurred.

Philippe Cuvier sat in the men's salon drinking steadily. It was clear now that Anna chose to be with the Italian, Donnelli. His ideas of having a New York Broadway star as his companion, living off her wealth—her jewels—or her income, was quickly vanishing into air. She had said nothing, but he fully expected her to tell him the next day that whatever they had was over.

In the far corner of the salon, he observed the Turk and the two Greeks in sometimes spirited, often surreptitious conversation. He wondered, with wry, mild curiosity, Are they putting together international plots, or just planning another liaison with traveling prostitutes?

Heggar Pasha glanced around the salon. No one present but the Frenchman in the corner. He motioned to the waiter for refills of their sweet Turkish wine and shortly raised his glass. "To tonight," he said. "The last night we can do what we must do."

The two Greeks held out their glasses and touched them to his. The one known as Demetrius said, "You must pay us in advance."

The Turk's lip twisted. "You Greeks. Thick, greedy . . ." His expression changed. "Not present company of course." He paused. "I pay half now. You are only a contingency. The other half—well, if I need your services, you will earn it well and get it then."

"You speak in circles." Argus exchanged a glance with Demetrius, who frowned deeply. "Why do you not say exactly what you expect?"

"In this car, I must be careful." He inclined his head toward the waiter against the far wall, and, beyond him, at the corner table, Cuvier. "There are too many ears here. We talk more in our rooms."

"Shall we go, then?"

The Pasha shook his head. "That compartment," he shuddered, "it has bad memories now."

Argus nodded. "Memories of the Pasha, or the woman who killed him?"

"Both. To think—an hour before, one of those women was in my arms, maybe the one who held the knife."

Argus asked, "Your government . . . You will be blamed for Ovar's death?"

The Pasha's forehead creased. "Only if I fail in what remains to be done. Tonight can make the difference."

They left the salon for their compartments. Demetrius walked slowly and held Argus back with an arm, allowing the Turk to move on ahead of them, out of earshot.

"The sweaty, rude arrogance of the man," he whispered to Argus. "He insults the Greek nation, and he insults us, day after day. I cannot take much more of this."

Argus said softly, "Our turn comes."

"I know. I cannot wait . . . Watch it, we are here."

*   *   *

General Klaus Eberhardt held Mata Hari close to him on the bed and caressed her soft hair. Pillows were propped up behind them. He wore pajamas and a robe, she a gown and peignoir. They sipped champagne.

"It's our last night," Eberhardt said. "Soon, we must go on our separate ways, where our duty takes us." He waited for a reaction, hoping he knew what it would be. His duty called, yes, but this woman— she had become as important to him as the tasks his superiors expected him to accomplish.

Mata Hari looked into his eyes. "We can have no truly separate ways after this trip, Klaus. I think you know that. Beneath your cold, German steel-plate hide, you have a warm, passionate heart."

He frowned. "But a man—a German—must keep that steel about him in these times, and in the days ahead. Our two countries will be at each other's throats, soon."

"But not us, my general." She pressed her moist lips on his. "We must go on, somehow. Don't you value love equally with war?"

"Yes I've used the word, as little as I understand its meaning. But I don't know—events are moving fast."

"An hour can be a lifetime. We must steal as many hours as we can from the world. For ourselves."

Klaus Eberhardt's second most powerful motive, attraction to women, had a way of taking over and pushing his life's work of war—the legitimized, systematic murder he was obsessed with—out of his thoughts, whenever his passion controlled. The young man he once was, before all of his military training, broke through in those moments and took over his feelings. At those times, Eberhardt could imagine he was simply young, blond-headed Klaus again—the youth who wanted nothing more than love.

He put their champagne glasses on the floor and pulled Mata Hari closer to him. His excitement rose as he felt her body against his own. And in their embrace, all thoughts of war and conspiracy soon left the General's mind.

Elizabeth and Tony Arnaud sat together looking out their window at the rain blowing against the glass. She felt at peace, believing the ultimate danger of the trip—the bomb—had been encountered and overcome. Ahead now lay their honeymoon, long languid days in the Greek Islands.

Afterward, they'd go home to her parents, surprise them with word of her marriage and their coming child. She resolved to send them a telegram from Bucharest and hint at the good news. A grandchild for them would soften their hearts toward Tony.

Tony said, "If that bomb had gone off on the train . . ."

"Shush," she said. "It's over."

"But our baby—it could have been killed before it was born."

"Darling. Everything is over—even the ghost. She seems to have gone, too."

He looked at her, frowning. "There's something about that I should tell you, and the Professor, before he leaves tomorrow. It is, how do you say it, on my conscience?"

"The Professor? Why him?"

"Remember," Tony said, "I told him about the apparition."

"It was I who told him, dear. I'm the one who saw her."

"I let him and M'sieur Bayard believe I did, also."
He paused. "And I didn't. I saw nothing."

"It doesn't matter."

"I let them think it, for money. That makes me
a thief."

She laughed. "You mean because we received a
refund of our fares? That bothers you?"

"I am not a thief. They must understand that."

"Don't worry. My father could pay ten times the
fare. If the Express wants us to have a free trip, what
harm is there in that? It makes Mr. Bayard feel better
that we don't talk about it to other passengers. We
kept our word."

He shook his head. "I think I should tell the Professor before he leaves the train at Bucharest. It would
release me from this burden."

Elizabeth's forehead creased. "There's no burden
on you, no reason to worry so much. I was the one
who talked to them. And it's all past now."

"You don't know everything about this."

"Maybe not. But, whatever you think, Tony, you
are not a thief." She put her lips close to his ear and
whispered, "Except, of course, for this—you have
stolen my heart."

Agatha Miller sat in bed at two a.m., her writing
folder on her lap, her pencil in hand. She wrote down
ideas that flowed faster than her pencil would move.
She crossed out words and wrote above them. Several pages filled with words lay on the bed. She finished the current page, ripped it from the pad, and
tossed it among the others.

The beginnings of her novel were taking shape.
She studied the idea in her mind, the setting she
would put in the book—a house in the English coun-
tryside. She smiled, realizing the description she was

writing of the gabled mansion was idealized, a place she dreamed of having herself, with a sitting room and a library overlooking gardens bursting with flowers.

The body lay on the green carpet, the young woman's face contorted, a wineglass lying near one outstretched hand. It had to be cyanide, naturally—as she experienced on this train. She touched the pencil to her lips as the characters in her book roamed through her mind—a doctor, a young girl, and a handsome boy who assisted the doctor.

Agatha Miller lay her head back against the pillow, inventing jealousies and secrets of the past among the relatives. She could see the mansion in her mind's eye, hear her characters' voices, talking, arguing, all mingled with the train's rumble, and the sound of the rain on her window. Her eyes closed, her arms relaxed, and the pencil slipped from her fingers. She drifted into dreams of a country house, which her imagination would despoil with an unexpected visit by death.

Chapter Twenty-Two

The relentless rain, accompanied occasionally by the cymbal sound of a thunderclap, provided a rhythmic lullaby for the passengers of the Orient Express. Even conductor Albert, who prided himself on being able to sit in the hard chair at the jog near the end of the corridor through the night without falling asleep, succumbed to it. His head tilted down on his chest and his breathing became heavy and regular. He did not see or hear the woman walking toward him, obviously intent on going to the water closet at the end of the corridor.

She walked purposefully, but wearing soft, satin slippers made no noticeable sound amid the noises of the rain and train. She held her loose pink peignoir together about her with one hand. In the other she held a packet of powders and a glass. She passed the conductor, let herself into the water closet, and closed the door. She checked her watch, which read 3:05 A.M.

Fifteen minutes later, Mata Hari returned to her compartment and carefully locked the door after her. She saw that the connecting door to General Eberhardt's room was closed, tested the knob, and found it locked. She climbed into bed, stared at the ceiling for long minutes, restive, sorting out conflicting feelings in her thoughts, but at last succumbed to the lure of sleep.

The Sunday morning regimen for passengers began at a more leisurely pace, with a champagne breakfast at nine a.m. The last day on the Express for many—those detraining at Bucharest—brought a spirit of poignancy as well as expectancy for the next legs of their various journeys. Some would remain in Bucharest for an extended stay, while others would return to Paris on the west-bound Express trip back in a few days. Others would continue to Constantinople, and beyond.

When Mata Hari failed to rouse the General by rapping, first softly, then more loudly, on their connecting door at 8:30 A.M., she sought out Albert. "Would you check on the General, Albert? You have the master key?"

He nodded. "What is wrong, madame?"

"I . . . I don't know. He doesn't answer my knock."

They walked back down the corridor, Albert in the lead.

Albert quickly opened General Eberhardt's door with his passkey and eased it ajar a few inches, calling out, "General? General Eberhardt?" He listened, but heard no sound, and peered in through the opening. He gasped and said, "No!" He put his arm back to shield Mata Hari, and pulled the door closed. "Miss Zelle, if you would please go and bring the Manager here."

"What is it? Tell me!"

"We must save the time. You go, I will see to this."

"No!" She pushed open the door and rushed into the room. As she neared the bed, she saw a knife hilt protruding from the General's chest. She put her hand to her mouth but could not stifle her scream entirely. She fell onto the bed and looked at the face of Klaus Eberhardt. His staring eyes seemed to glare at the ceiling. "Oh, God! Klaus, Klaus!" Her sobs filled the room.

"I go then, Miss Zelle," Albert said. "You stay here. But let no one in." He rushed through the doorway, allowing the door to bang shut behind him. Two minutes later, he found Bayard in the kitchen and poured the story out in his native French, Bayard answering in kind. As Bayard ran toward the General's compartment, Albert followed to that point, then continued on to Darnell's door and pounded on it, as Bayard instructed.

John Darnell and Penny were dressed and preparing to go to the dining car. Hearing a knock on the door, he opened it with the thought that it was an announcement of breakfast, the time being almost nine a.m., but was instead greeted by Albert's distraught face. Albert told him in breathless, disjointed words of the knife in General Eberhardt's chest, and urged Darnell to hurry with him to compartment one, where Bayard awaited him.

Darnell turned to Penny, who had listened to the exchange. "You go on to breakfast. I'll join you in a while." Moments later, he burst through the General's doorway and over to the bed, where Mata Hari sat with a numb expression on her face, her eyes red and tear-filled. He glanced at Bayard, who bit at a fingernail and stared at the body.

Darnell stepped up to the bedside. He closed the eyelids of the General. He looked at the knife hilt and frowned. The General's Luger lay on the floor. He picked it up and sniffed the barrel. "Not fired," he said.

He turned to Mata Hari. "You should go to your own quarters," he said, "away from all this . . . Pierre?" He nodded toward the connecting door, his eyes telling Bayard what to do with the distraught woman.

Bayard took her arm and brought her to a standing position. "This way, please, madame." He took her to the door, unlocked it, and walked her through the doorway into her room. "Please, just sit here for a while. We'll be back soon."

She nodded and hung her head in her hands. She sobbed into her handkerchief as Bayard returned to Darnell's side.

Darnell looked up at Bayard from his crouched position as he examined the body. "This knife, Pierre. Do you see?"

"What?"

"It's the same kind of knife that killed Ovar Pasha."

"You say, the same knife?"

"No, but very similar. It has the same long, leather hilt. And the silver crossbar."

"But—the prostitute? She killed the Pasha. She's not on the train—it could not be her."

"I agree. But the question really is, if such a woman killed the Pasha, how can the knives be the same, since she has left the train?"

"She could have used a knife she found in the Turks' compartment."

Darnell nodded. "Yes. That's reasonable. No doubt Heggar Pasha will tell us that. But where did this knife come from?"

Bayard seemed to suddenly absorb the full impact of the scene. *"Mon Dieu!* This is the third death on my train! How will my Board react—three murders, and a bomb?"

"You killed no one, Pierre. And you could not prevent the murders, nor do anything about the bomb." He paused. "But yes, we have had three murders now—I think we can agree on that. You'll be unable to continue to call the death of Major Coulton a suicide any longer."

Bayard nodded. "But why all these killings?"

"We have until Bucharest to find out. The police there will swarm all over the train. A German general has been brutally murdered, Pierre, and that's serious. News of it will travel like the wind all the way to Berlin." He thought a bit. "We'll leave the body here. The police will want to inspect the scene."

"And the woman?" He looked over toward Mata Hari's room.

Darnell nodded at the connecting door. "Tell her we're locking that door and his corridor door, and that she should not enter this room. I'll be back soon to speak with her."

Bayard did as he said, and, when they left, Bayard posted Albert at the corridor door. "Stay here, Albert. No one is to enter the General's compartment," he said, "except the Professor or myself." The conductor nodded in assent.

"Let's find Heggar Pasha, now," Darnell said. "I have some questions to ask him."

Penny Darnell sat next to Madame Morgana and opposite Tony and Elizabeth Arnaud in the dining room. She sipped coffee, but turned around every few minutes to look at the door.

"Your husband will be here soon," the Madame said.

Penny smiled. "I hope so. Is that a prediction?"

Elizabeth said, "He couldn't be far. I know he didn't pass through the dining car."

"Perhaps with the Manager, *n'est-ce pas*?" Tony said.

Elizabeth laid a hand on Penny's. "Look—here he comes."

Penny turned and stood, dropping her napkin on the table. As Darnell approached, she reached out her hands to him. "John—what is it?"

"I can't tell you just now. Go ahead and have breakfast. I have some important things to do. I'll be back."

Bayard stepped through the doorway and over to the table where the Turk and the two Greeks sat drinking black coffee.

Darnell said to Penny, "I'll return as soon as I can." He walked back to the Turk's table and joined Bayard.

"Good morning," Heggar Pasha said, looking up at Darnell. He turned to Bayard. "The Express should serve Turkish coffee. This weak imitation—"

Darnell cut him off. "We're not here to speak of coffee, Heggar. Shall we go to your room for privacy—or talk here?"

The Pasha frowned. "And why would we need the privacy? Say what you will." His gaze was unswerving.

Darnell wanted reaction from his next words, so he let them come out bluntly. "General Eberhardt was stabbed to death last night by a knife exactly like the one that killed Ovar Pasha in your room."

Heggar Pasha did not blink. "Another death, what a tragedy." He paused. "A lover's quarrel, perhaps?"

"The knife—like the one we found in Ovar's chest. You have no comment on that?"

"You turned that one over to the police, I believe."

"And you had another?"

"No. Only the one. But they are not rare. I purchased that one—the one the lady of the night used on Ovar—at a shop at the station in Paris."

"Again—you had no others like it?"

"No."

"And you disclaim knowledge of this murder?"

"Of course I do. Now I ask you—do you accuse me?" The Pasha frowned, his eyes narrowed. "Be careful you do not reach too far, Professor."

The Greek Demetrius said, "We did not leave our compartment last night. It was neither Argus nor myself." He looked at Argus, who nodded. "We can vouch for each other."

Darnell stood. "This isn't over." He motioned to Bayard, who followed him as he walked through the doorway back into the sleeping car. Inside, the two of them alone, he said, "We must see Mata Hari now. I think she'll have something to say."

Minutes later they were at the door of compartment two.

"Albert's gone," Bayard said. "Will we need him?"

"No. I want to hear what this woman says. She's been holding back."

Darnell rapped on the door once, twice, before Mata Hari opened it. She held a handkerchief to her eyes, turned back into the room, and said, "Come in." She sat on the still unmade bed.

"I am sorry for your loss," Darnell said, as he and Bayard stepped into the compartment.

She began to cry anew, but in moments stifled her sobs and said, "I must get control of myself."

"He meant much to you."

She nodded, and said in a choked voice, "I-I loved him. I know it now." She looked up at him. "Why do you have to lose someone . . . ?"

". . . to know how much they mean to you? It's

one of the mysteries of the ages." Darnell gave her
a minute to compose herself. "There are things we
must ask you."

"I know . . . and things I must tell you. I've had
time to think. But where to start?" She paused. "We
met, the General and I, in a Paris hotel. He introduced me to some of his friends in the high com-
mands. They asked me—actually, paid me, I have to
admit that now—to go with him on this trip and
help him obtain a certain document or paper they
wanted."

Darnell interrupted. "Something Major Coulton
was carrying?"

"Yes. What they didn't know is, that I was already
working for the French government. They had assigned me to follow the General."

"An *agent double*," Bayard said.

She nodded. "What *I* didn't know is that I would
become so emotionally involved with Klaus."

Darnell said, "In this case, very ironic. But it happens, often, on trains, on ships. That's how I met
my wife."

"I knew I could not prevent what Klaus did, not
entirely, and my feelings became mixed, and confused." Again, she touched her handkerchief to her
eyes, which filled with tears.

"What did the General do?"

"He gave the cyanide powder to Ovar Pasha and
paid him to poison the Major and get the Major's
briefcase for him. I . . . well, I didn't find that out
until afterward. When the Pasha brought the Major's
case to Klaus, Klaus removed the document he was
seeking. I saw him do that. But I didn't see him put
the bomb in the Major's case. I didn't know about that
until later, when Klaus was talking loudly with the
Turk and I overheard them through our connecting

door. I wasn't a very good double agent, I'm afraid."
She looked at Darnell. "When you took the case into
the fields and it exploded, I realized it must have
been Klaus who planted the bomb in it."

"It would have exploded in Budapest, at the British Embassy, if Major Coulton had reached there
with it."

Bayard sank down onto a chair, saying nothing,
apparently numb with the revelations.

Darnell went on questioning her. "Let's talk about
Ovar Pasha. He was a German sympathizer, wasn't
he?"

"Yes, and a mercenary, and a paid assassin."

"The apparent attempt to poison the General—that
was a pretense, wasn't it? I see that now."

"The General thought it would divert suspicion
from himself."

"Did you know the Pashas tried to poison the
Prince at the party?"

"How—? Yes, I learned that later."

"I saw the Turk try it. What do you know about
it?"

"Klaus said the Prince carried news of a treaty
which in war could make Rumanian oil fields available to the British and French."

"Yes. I know that."

"The morning after the party, when the attempt to
poison Prince Carol failed, and we heard of Ovar
Pasha's death, Klaus admitted he had paid Ovar to
kill the Prince. Klaus complained, now his money
was gone, stolen from the Pasha by the women, and
he was angry the plan did not succeed. But, of
course, I was happy it failed."

"I don't believe a woman killed the Pasha. I think
that was a cover-up."

She nodded. "Heggar Pasha killed Ovar *after* the

women left the train. The Greeks were drugged. Heggar said he allowed the women to steal Ovar's money, using the theft as a cover to kill him. He said he did it to help France—I was a fool!''

Darnell frowned. "And the paper?"

"Heggar Pasha wanted to retrieve it from the General, who had taken it from the Major's case. Heggar told me it would be important to France, if it was kept out of German hands. He urged me to help him get it back."

"How?"

She took a deep, shivering breath. "This is where everything went wrong. His plan was . . . well, last night, he told me to leave my compartment for fifteen minutes, my door unlocked, and the connecting door between my room and the General's also open. Heggar would simply enter, retrieve the paper, and leave. He promised me Klaus would not be harmed. I insisted upon that."

Darnell said, "So you leave your room, Heggar Pasha enters through your door, crosses into the General's compartment, rifles the suitcases and briefcases, the General awakes and pulls out his gun. Heggar stabs him, before he can fire it."

"I think so. But the Pasha promised me . . ." The tears came again.

"The promise of a murderer is worth little."

Bayard seemed to come to life for a minute. "Who wrote the note, warning of the bomb?"

"You did, didn't you?" Darnell asked her, already knowing the answer.

"Yes. I was worried about the Prince, and, of course, about everyone on the train."

"And where is this mysterious paper, document, whatever it is?"

"I don't know."

Darnell stood. "Perhaps it could still be in the General's compartment. Heggar Pasha was interrupted when the General awoke and pulled out his Luger, and might have left after killing him, before finishing his search."

"Then he'll try to get it again," Bayard said.

Darnell offered another word of condolence to Mata Hari and the two men left the compartment.

"Now the General's compartment," Darnell said. "Your key?"

Bayard inserted the key in the closed door, but said, "It's unlocked!"

Darnell brushed by him and tried the General's door. It swung open at his touch.

Chapter Twenty-Three

The General's compartment was in complete disarray. "Damn!" Darnell said. "The Turk must have gotten here earlier, before us."

"He must have taken the General's key when he killed him." Bayard glanced about the room. "Where's the General's briefcase?"

"It's gone. Quick—to the Turk's room!" Darnell ran from the room, followed by the Manager. A minute later they stood at the Turk's compartment door. Darnell tried it, and found it was locked.

"Unlock it," Darnell told Bayard. "No time for ceremony."

Bayard opened it with his passkey and Darnell entered first, Bayard following.

Heggar Pasha turned and straightened up in surprise from examining the General's briefcase. "What . . . ?"

"We'll take that." Darnell leveled his .38 special at the Pasha's chest. "Get it, Bayard."

Bayard stepped forward and picked up the case from the table. He snapped it shut and moved back behind Darnell with it.

"So it's all over," Darnell said.

"Hah! Not quite. This is not a classroom, Professor. There are two things you do not know."

"I'm listening."

"We are both on the same side. Events are in planning that could precipitate the war many are waiting for. I don't want that. You don't want it. And your friend, the Prince, of a nation potentially friendly to Britain—I saved his life after that crude attempt by my foolish compatriot. He would have tried again, and succeeded next time."

Darnell ignored the speech. "Let's not try to deceive each other. I know you killed Ovar and the General."

The Turk rushed on. "Rumania can be a valuable ally to Britain and France in the coming war. It has extensive oil fields. Treaties can secure those for our allies."

"That makes murder acceptable?"

"Call it murder, if you will. I did not mean to kill the General."

"You're saying—what exactly?"

"He was the guilty one—using my misguided friend for his own murderous purposes—murdering the Major, and almost assassinating the Prince. Ovar had his justice coming."

"My dear Heggar. You forget two things. First, I sat at the head of the table and was able to observe you and Ovar when you stood in front of the Prince. It was *your* hand that dropped the powders into the Prince's glass, not *Ovar's* hand."

"Damn you, infidel!"

"I've talked with Mata Hari, who has implicated you in the murders of both Ovar and the General. You'll have a lot to explain to the Bucharest police. They have an unbroken record of obtaining confessions. And the General's death will give another edge to all this in Germany. A very sharp edge."

The Turk stared at him, and for the first time, Darnell saw genuine fear in the man's eyes. Was it the reference to the Bucharest police methods? Or to Germany?

Darnell turned to Bayard. "We need to lock him up."

Heggar Pasha smirked. "You haven't asked, Professor, about the other thing you don't know."

Darnell's eyes narrowed, and for some inexplicable reason his pulse began to race. This Pasha had a final card to play.

Heggar Pasha's oily voice sent shivers down Darnell's spine. "Have you talked with your lovely wife lately?"

Darnell turned to Bayard and said urgently, "I have to find Penny! Get some men in here."

Bayard rushed into the hall and in moments brought back two conductors. When he came back in, Darnell said, "Hold him here," and ran out of the room.

He burst into their own compartment and saw that Penny was not there. He rushed through the dining room to the ladies' salon.

Madame Morgana sat at a table, writing. Answering his breathless question, she said, "After breakfast, we came in here. One of the Greeks stopped by— Demetrius, I think—and told Penny you had asked that she come to you. I don't know where they went."

Darnell ran back through the first-class car, into second class, and on to the Greeks' room. The door was unlocked and no one there. Just then, Albert walked up to him, hatless, his collar askew, and rubbing his head.

"Someone hit me," Albert said. "I woke on the floor in the storage closet."

"Have you seen my wife?"

"She passed me a few minutes before I was attacked—walking that way, with one of the Greeks." He pointed to the caboose.

Darnell whirled and ran to the caboose, gun in his right hand. He pounded on the locked door and shouted, "Open the door!"

When it opened, he was surprised to find Penny standing in front of him, holding it open. She put her hand on his. "It's all right, John. They were protecting me."

He looked past her to see Demetrius and Argus standing there, smiling, hands in the air. Cautious, he entered the room and closed the door behind him, still holding his .38 at the ready.

"Tell him, Demetrius," Penny said.

"Professor, you can lower your gun. We are your friends."

"I'm waiting for you to explain why you kidnapped my wife." He still held the gun ready.

Demetrius continued. "First, we must tell you we were assigned to this train by our superiors in Athens to deal with these Turks. To watch them. We've done this before. This time, the main object was to keep them from harming the Prince. We knew he was traveling on the Express."

"Your superiors—they suspected the Turks of planning an assassination of the Prince?"

"We knew they'd try something. We were aware of Ovar's leanings. We knew of General Eberhardt, and the kind of work he was assigned to." Demetrius looked to the other Greek for concurrence, and Argus nodded.

"Go on."

"We put ourselves in the midst of the two Turks," Demetrius said, "in the next compartment. They trusted us, from previous times we had traveled on conveyances, watching them. The drinking, the card playing, the women—we had to endure all that. All in the line of duty—but distasteful, of course."

"Of course."

"Then after Ovar was killed—we suspected Heggar killed him—we were relieved. We thought Heggar shared our loyalty to the Prince." Demetrius and Argus lowered their arms.

"You were wrong about Heggar, but so were others. Go on."

Argus spoke up. "Heggar said he planned to rifle the General's room, and was worried something might go wrong. He wanted, as he put it, insurance."

Demetrius nodded. "He paid us to take your wife hostage, to protect him."

Darnell said grimly, "Which you did."

Demetrius shook his head. "No. Not as a hostage for *him*. Not for his reasons. You say he is not what we thought he was. Even so, either way, we do not believe in kidnapping or murder to achieve even the most honorable ends. And—it is an old cultural feeling—we do not like or trust Turks, at least this one."

"So we brought her here," Argus said, "and explained to her we would protect her until you arrived. Keep her safe from the Pasha, who had already killed two people. We knew you would appear."

"You were protecting her from Heggar?"

"Exactly."

Darnell looked at Penny. She nodded.

Penny touched Darnell's arm. "Now will you put

that ugly gun away?" She pushed his gun hand down toward the floor. "And let's get out of here, please."

Darnell stepped over to the Greeks and shook their hands. "Thank you. I'm in your debt."

He took Penny's arm and they left the car. He stopped in the hallway and held her. "I was worried, Penny. I need to know you're secure until we reach Bucharest." His look was grim. "There's one last thing I have to do."

After securing Penny in their compartment and cautioning her not to open the door except to himself, Darnell returned to the Turk's compartment. He found Bayard and the two conductors standing facing the Turk, who sat at the window table.

"Your wife?" Bayard looked at Darnell, eyes questioning.

Darnell glared at Heggar Pasha. "My wife is just fine."

The Turk's expression was wooden, but his eyes showed surprise.

"What now?" Bayard asked.

"Now I examine the General's briefcase." He handed his .38 to Bayard. "Hold this on him."

Darnell took the case and set it on the bed behind the others, out of view of the Turk.

The lock on the case had been forced open. He snapped open the catches and lifted the lid. Numerous papers and envelopes enscripted in the German language were strewn on top. He riffled through them quickly and tossed them aside on the bed. In the bottom of the case, a large white envelope bore the words, written in a bold hand in English, "British Embassy."

He tore open the envelope. He removed the single

sheet of British watermarked paper inside and looked at it.

The words on it had been written in the center of the page on a typewriter, in capital letters, on every second line. He read the words to himself, a warning of a scheme threatening a "young world leader." He pursed his lips and gave a low, silent whistle. The words recalled the ominous predictions of Madame Morgana in the quatrains she spoke at the party for the Prince. Her words flashed in his mind again— *fall of a youthful leader*. Could this note somehow refer to Prince Carol? He folded the sheet and put it and the envelope in his inner coat pocket.

"We'll have to tie him up," Darnell said. "Have your men get something to tie him with, and keep him in here. When do we reach Bucharest?"

Bayard glanced at his watch and answered, "Two hours."

"He'll keep that long."

Darnell retrieved his gun from Bayard, and as he left the room, he heard Bayard instructing Albert to go to the storeroom in search of rope.

Chapter Twenty-Four

Mata Hari held Madame Morgana's hands tightly in both of hers. "I had to talk with you. Is it all right?"

The Madame looked across her compartment table at the tear-streaked face of the other woman. "Of course, my dear. The General—you were very close to him, weren't you?" She patted the other's hand gently before withdrawing hers.

"I loved him. Like no one else I ever knew. We were so opposite in many ways—he was German and a military man."

"And you are French, Miss Zelle? And, of course, a dancer."

"I am Dutch. I was born in Holland. Margaretha Geertruuda Zelle. But I've lived and performed in France for years."

The Madame smiled. "You have another stage name."

"It's no secret any longer. Mata Hari."

"It was never a secret to me. The 'eye of the day.' "

"Yes—I heard you say that at dinner. You knew."

"I had no reason to acknowledge it, if you wanted it kept secret . . . but now, with all this happening, you must admit it to the police."

Mata Hari nodded. "Nothing matters anymore."

The psychic shook her head vigorously. "On the contrary, everything matters. You are alive. You have your life to live."

"That's why I'm here. I-I know you see the future. Can you look into it for me? I must know . . ."

She frowned. "It is almost always better we do not know what is around the next corner."

"I must know."

"Why?"

"You say I should go on living. But is life worth living? In two years I will be forty. In Malay, I lost my young son, just a baby, not even three years old. He and my other baby were poisoned by our own nursemaid—only the baby girl lived. Now my General is dead."

"You still have your daughter."

"We are not close—it's because of my life, you must know. It pushes her away from me."

The Madame's face was expressionless. "You are determined to know your future?"

She nodded tearfully. "Yes."

Madame Morgana rose and went to her larger suitcase. She took out a dark mirror and propped it up in front of Mata Hari's face. "There is no guarantee. I have no magic wand. But, look into this dark reflective glass, while I speak."

Mata Hari stared into the black glass, seeing her reflection staring back at her. "I am ready."

The Madame's voice began softly, monotonously. "You are looking backward, first, backward at your own life. You will see faces, remembered faces from the past, other faces you have forgotten, but which are still in your mind . . ." Her words droned on and on.

Mata Hari heard the words seep into her mind. In the glass—or was it in her mind's eye?—she saw her baby boy, Norman, smiling . . . her daughter, as she appeared the last time she saw her, at fifteen years of age . . . her husband, Lord MacLeoud, when she left him, and the General's face, his forehead creased with worry.

She struggled against the memories.

"You will now look at the future, at faces you will find ahead, things you will do in your life, things you would like to do."

The Madame's words brought new visions—horses running across a wild field, books of poetry, faces of men without features. A knife, dripping with blood, flashed across her field of vision, and she seemed to hear many rifles firing. If she had been in a somnolent state, the sound in her mind snapped her back to reality and her lips parted as she tried to scream. She jerked up to a standing position and put a hand over her mouth.

"Softly, softly," the Madame said. She rested an arm around the other's shoulder. "It's all right—you must tell me what you saw."

Mata Hari told the Madame of the visions, but said she could not connect the future with the present.

The Madame nodded. "As I said, it is better sometimes to know nothing of the future. But now that you know this much—"

"Yes? What does it mean?"

"It's clear you like horses and poetry. Your life ahead could be filled with them. But you must be very careful. There is danger on certain paths."

"More danger?" She trembled. "Then I'll return to France, where I've always felt safe. I'll live in the country, and, yes, have some horses, and write poetry. A simple life." She paused. "But what dangers could be worse than my General's death?"

Madame Morgana scowled and stared out the window at the passing fields and trees. The rain had resumed and obscured a clear view of the country-side. "Your own death," she said. "The dark mirror shows the dark side of one's life. You spoke of a knife, and guns. Those are warnings—you must guard against any more dangerous involvements. They could be your undoing."

Anna Held finished packing her suitcases and snapped them shut. She had glanced in her jewelry box and selected one of her simpler necklaces with a matching bracelet to wear as she left the train.

Her plan was to check into her hotel, with Anton Donnelli occupying an adjoining room, as he was now, next to her. The connecting door was locked at the moment, but she intended to open it soon, so they could spend the last hour or so together on the train, and talk of their plans.

A rap on the corridor door came at that moment. She stepped over to open it and found Philippe Cu-vier standing there with a dour expression on his face.

"May I come in?"

She stood aside. After he entered, she closed the door and leaned back against it. She thought she knew what he would say.

"It is good-bye, is it not?" He looked at her from the far side of the room.

She breathed heavily. Was her corset too tight? Her back bothered her. "Yes, Philippe. What we had in Paris . . ."

"We lost it. I know that."

"What will you do?"

He shrugged. "My home is in Bucharest. I have my business." He stepped across the room and took both of her hands. "But I will miss you." He kissed her lightly on both cheeks. "And now I go. But if you ever need anything, call me." At the door, he looked back and said, "I hope your life will be happy."

When the door closed, Anna sank down on the bed and dried inexplicable tears from her eyes. Was she doing the right thing?

She picked up her Pomeranian and stroked his head over and over. "Henri, Henri, these decisions of the heart are so hard." Determinedly, she took a deep breath and stepped back to the connecting door to Anton Donnelli's compartment. She knocked on the door lightly. Awaiting a reply from the man who could be a big part of her future, she stood there holding her golden-orange dog, cradled in her arms, as if he were her baby.

Anton Donnelli opened the door and smiled at the woman before him. He had grown to care deeply for Anna Held in these few days on the train. To be with her, be part of her life, and make her part of his, would mean giving up his livelihood, his entire means of income—stealing and selling jewels. He wondered what kind of work he could do beyond that.

"Good morning, my dear Anna." He broadened his smile. "And Henri." He stepped aside and waved an arm. "Come in, please. I have some champagne here."

As Anna Held walked toward him, he reached out and embraced her. He guided her toward the table where an open champagne bottle and fluted glasses waited. He filled the glasses and lifted his to hers. "To our new adventures in Bucharest."

She nodded. "And to the Orient Express—which introduced us to each other."

They sat next to each other at the table. Anna put her dog down on the floor and took Anton's hand. "I look forward to seeing how you live in your home, after a few days in the hotel."

His forehead wrinkled, and at that moment he knew he must dispose of the burden he had been carrying on his mind for several days. "Anna—I—I—have something important to tell you. Something painful."

"Painful for me?"

"Perhaps for you, yes. But more painful for me. I have a confession to make."

She held a hand to her mouth. "You're . . . married?"

He smiled, relieved to have that respite. "No, no, no. There is only you. But—there is no way of softening what I have to say, Anna. I am—at least, I have been—a thief. And my name is not Anton Donnelli. It is Arturo Donatello."

Anna Held's eyes widened. She set down her glass and stared into his eyes. "A thief? Are you—wanted by the law?"

He shook his head. "Not officially. No one knows of my past—well, just one person, a reliable one, on this train—but not the police. I have escaped that." He took her hands in his. "But I want you to know, I've given it up. I'll never steal again. Never!"

Her hand crept up to her throat and the necklace around her neck. "What . . . what did you steal?"

"I think you know. Diamonds, jewelry."

"You were going to steal my jewels?"

His forehead knotted. "I'll tell you everything. Your jewels are safe now. But, before I became . . . close to you, I took them. Later, with the help of someone, I put them back."

Her sharp intake of breath disturbed him. "Please, Anna—it's all over. You've changed my life, I swear.

The way I've learned to feel for you has made a thief into an honest man for the first time in twenty years. Can you forgive me?"

Tears streamed down her face as she looked at him. She said nothing for a moment. She reached into his topcoat pocket and removed the white handkerchief, held it to her eyes. She looked out the window, as if searching for an answer there, and at last faced him again.

"You stole my jewels . . . but you put the jewelry back—worth many thousands of dollars, all that I have left of value really from America. What if you had kept them? And then, you also stole my heart. What is the truth? I don't know. Anton—Arturo—it is so much to put on me."

"I made a mistake. But you can trust me now. Spend a week with me in Bucharest. After that, you can decide for both of us what we should do. But I promise I will be honest with the law."

"No more stealing?"

"Never."

She sighed deeply. "What can I say to a man who cares for me enough to give me back all I own of value, to confess, to tell me everything, and give up his whole way of life?"

"Say yes." He took her in his arms. "Will you?"

Anna Held said nothing. But she embraced him.

Darnell stopped at General Eberhardt's compartment. A conductor, on guard, let him into the room. He stepped inside and walked to the bed, where the General's body still lay. The room was cold, and he had the sensation of being in a funeral parlor. Only the flowers were missing.

He stopped short at the bed and stared at the General's body with surprise. The knife last seen in his chest was missing now. Did Bayard take it? And if he did, why would he do that?

He looked about the room and examined the contents of the suitcases once more but found no knife, and nothing else of interest. He pulled the bedsheet up and over the General's face. He left the room, locking the door again from the corridor side. He hurried to his own compartment, anxious to get away from the face of death, to be with Penny, and just hold her close.

Agatha Miller gazed across the dining room table and the two coffee cups the waiter had filled for them. She smiled at Donald Brand. "It's been an exciting trip, Donald. I'm almost sorry to see it end."

"Almost?"

"Yes. Because life has to move forward, just as in a novel. You meet characters, you live through an experience, and then you go on to the next."

"So, I'm a character, am I?"

"Yes. And one of the nicest ones I've known."

"And now what? We end the chapter, close the book—to use your expressions?"

She looked out the window, and with the sunlight creeping through now, her hair shone in a burnished copper hue. "I don't know what my entire future holds. I'm not a Madame Morgana, able to see ahead. But I have my nursing assignment, and I have to fulfill that. I *am* a nurse, you know. And you know I'm betrothed. I marry this year. And then . . . I don't know."

He frowned. "How long will you be in Bucharest?"

"Two months, at the most, three. Then back to England."

"I go back, too, after I wrap up my duties here, and make deliveries to Budapest." His smooth brow creased. "But you must sense how I feel about you."

She shook her head. "No, Donald, that's just traveler's romantic fever. It will pass. One must keep one's commitments. I have mine, and you've always known that." Her jaw was firm.

He looked down. "This trip, all of it, was in vain."

"Don't be so somber. Think of the tales you'll have to tell your superiors. How you walked about with that bomb in your case for days, not knowing it. How you carried on under extremely grim circumstances after the Major died."

"That's true." He brightened. "Maybe—I don't know—they might make me a senior courier."

"You see? We learn from experiences in different ways. This trip inspired me to travel to the East—Alexandria, Constantinople, Baghdad. And I've gotten ideas and notes for my books—spies, murder, cyanide."

Donald Brand smiled. He held up his coffee cup toward hers. "Then let's drink to the mysteries of the renowned author, Agatha Miller!"

In the quiet of the room, the clink of their coffee cups made an unusually cheerful sound, and the two waiters at the end of the room smiled at each other as they watched from their respectful distance. The sun streamed through the windows now, and the cheerfulness of it matched the room's mood.

Chapter Twenty-Five

Darnell took Penny in his arms. "It's all over, darling. The Turk is in custody, and we reach Bucharest in one hour. We'll stay a few nights, then head back to Paris."

"I was worried about you."

He touched her lips with his. "You always worry, and it's always needless."

"Well . . . so we'll get to see *la Tour Eiffel* from the top this time?" She made a triangle with the fingers of her two hands in the shape of the tower.

"The very top."

"Then we'd better do our packing."

He nodded and snapped open their suitcases. He watched Penny move gracefully around the room, in a kind of dance, picking up this and that article of clothing, laying them in the suitcases. Mata Hari could learn a few steps from her, he thought, smiling.

As he pulled on his coat, he felt the bulge of a book in one pocket. He slipped it out and glanced at it. He must look through it before returning it to Tony Arnaud. But a loud pounding on their door interrupted him, and he replaced it in his pocket. Darnell jumped up and pulled the door open.

Bayard collapsed into the room, blood dripping

from one sleeve. An ugly red gash on his forehead bled down onto his face. "The . . . the Pasha . . . he's escaped!"

Darnell helped him over to a chair. "Some water, Penny," he urged. He took Bayard's handkerchief from his pocket and wiped blood from the man's face. "What happened—quickly!"

Bayard took a breath. "He had a gun—a small one—taped to his arm, up a sleeve. When Albert left to get some rope to tie him, there were just two of us left—the other conductor and I—and, suddenly, the gun was pointed at us."

"Then?"

"He hit the conductor and ordered me to give him my master key. I grabbed him, and he shot me in the arm—here. He hit the back of my neck. I remember nothing then until I woke."

"How long were you unconscious?"

"A few minutes—I don't know."

"The Prince!" Darnell shouted. "He's after the Prince!"

He said to Penny, "Take care of him. Lock the door." He pulled out his .38 and charged into the hall running forward, into the dining car.

Chef Voisseron stopped him as he neared the door to the Prince's private car. "Wait! He's in there," he said, pointing to the door. "He rushed by here. He was waving a gun at the passengers. *Mon Dieu!*"

"Give me your key. Your master key—you have one?"

"No. But Albert—"

Darnell ran over to Albert, who stood staring at the door to the private car. "Your master key, Albert, quick."

The conductor fumbled in a pocket and produced the key. "But you can't go in there, sir."

"I'm not going in this way. I'm going over the top of the train to the tender car. Come and help me get on the roof."

The two ran back to the connection between the dining car and first-class car and Albert opened the outer door. "This ladder on the car will get you up there, sir."

Darnell looked out at the metal ladder built into the side of the dining car. He buttoned his coat tightly, put the .38 into a side pocket, and swung out onto the ladder. He was surprised at the force of the wind that greeted him.

Smoke and soot particles assaulted him in the rushing wind, and the wheel noises were magnified to an extent he had not realized existed outside the comfort of the coaches. He climbed up the ladder one step at a time, holding tightly in the wind. At the top, he sized up the surface of the car. It looked relatively flat, but there were no handholds, and the car swayed from side to side.

He pulled himself up to the top and walked slowly with legs outstretched and arms waving to balance himself. After a few steps, he was able to judge his balance better, and he moved forward methodically, with his head down to keep the smoke and soot out of his eyes. He passed over the dining car, onto the private car, where he stepped slowly, so as not to make noticeable noise below. When he reached the tender car, he had another thought, and walked over the top of it to the engine. He swung down into the cab behind the surprised engineer, Able Duncan. Sandy Porter, the fireman, was also on duty.

"Hello, men," he said, and took what amusement he could from their startled expressions.

"Professor! My God!" Duncan's eyes were wide.

"I need your help, men," Darnell said. "The Prince's life may depend on it."

He explained the situation of the Turk in the Prince's private car in a few terse words, then asked the engineer, "What's the road ahead like, Able?"

"It's a straightaway for a mile or two, then there's a long curve."

Darnell put his hand on Able's shoulder. "Here's what I want you to do. When we come to the curve, you would naturally slow down, correct?"

"Yes, sir. Either that or the train would leave the track."

"All right. Take it around the curve at a safe speed; the long curve will unsettle the man a bit. Then when you reach the straightaway again, speed up. He will relax, feel you're heading forward again. Then hit the brakes."

Able's eyes seemed to register understanding. "Catch him off guard."

"Exactly."

"I'll do it."

"Good. I'm counting on you."

Darnell worked his way around the tender, step by step, holding on to a railing, metal steps, whatever he could grasp. At the far end, he saw that the door to the Prince's private car had a small window similar to the one at the other end.

Staying to one side to avoid being seen, he glanced quickly through the glass then ducked down again. In that instant, he saw Heggar Pasha standing, faced away from the door, toward the Prince and Zizi, who were seated. Behind the Prince a few paces sat his two aides. The Pasha held his gun aimed at the Prince and seemed to be talking to him.

Darnell felt the train slow and move slightly to the left as Able Duncan took it into the long curve. For what seemed minutes the train swayed in the direction of the curve, but at last Darnell felt it begin to straighten again and speed up. He glanced in the window again and saw all were in their same positions. Softly, he slipped the master key into the lock, keeping his hand on it. The train was back to full speed now, and he prepared himself.

Now the brakes hit, and Darnell held to the door handle to keep from being thrown forward, turned the key, and burst into the car. As he did so, Heggar Pasha tumbled backward toward him, and their paths collided, the Pasha's gun bouncing across the carpeted floor.

Darnell unleashed a hard blow at the chin of the unprepared, disoriented Turk, propelling him across the room into the window. He heard the man's head crack against the glass.

He charged forward and again struck the Pasha with all his force. The man crumpled and slid down the wall to the floor, groaning, blood spurting from his lip.

Picking up the Turk's gun, he leveled it at the man and said, "Move and you're dead. Now, lie flat on the floor, head and face down, and put your hands behind your back." He dropped the Turk's gun into his pocket and took out his own .38.

He pulled off the Turk's belt and tied the man's hands together with it. He remembered what Bayard had said about the concealed gun. He checked the man's arms, legs, and body for any concealed weapons and found nothing this time.

"Thank God, Professor!" The Prince came over to him and pulled him in with his arms. "Excuse the embrace—but I was afraid Zizi and I would not live out this day."

"I'll get this trash out of your way," Darnell said. "Get up, Heggar."

The man tried to rise and Darnell assisted by pulling up on the belted hands.

"Let's go."

As Darnell walked by Zizi Lambrino, she moved forward, threw an arm around him, pulled him to her, and kissed Darnell on the cheek. "We can't thank you enough. We owe you our lives."

Darnell smiled, flustered, saying, "Of course, of course, my pleasure." But as he walked into the dining car, he thought of the word he'd used speaking to Zizi. *Pleasure?* He shook his head. The only true pleasure would be alighting at Bucharest with Penny—and finally putting this trip behind them.

Chapter Twenty-Six

As Darnell entered the dining room, the voices of Bayard, the chef, cooks, and passengers all rose in unison, saying words like "Thank God!" and "He's got 'im." Two of the cooks broke into applause. He saw Penny standing with Agatha Miller by a table in the back of the room.

Pierre Bayard, his arm bandaged, met Darnell as he moved forward into the room. Bayard motioned to Albert and a second conductor to come over, and said to Darnell, "Once again, my friend, you save us. We'll take this over now."

Albert produced a length of rope from his pocket and tied the Turk's arms more securely behind him.

Bayard said, "We'll tie him hand and foot in the caboose this time. No more escapes. We're not far from Bucharest now."

Darnell handed the Turk's gun to Bayard. "Keep your hands on this. I made sure he has no other weapons."

Bayard nodded at the conductors. "Bring him along." He strode purposefully through the first-class car doorway, the conductors following, each holding an arm of the Turk, who still looked dazed.

Penny ran forward to Darnell and into his arms. "Just hold me. Don't say anything."

Darnell did as he was told, but minutes later as they sat at a table, he found himself answering a dozen questions about what he did, and how he did it, and why he continued to risk his life. And at last the tears began to flow from her eyes.

Darnell and Penny spent an hour in their compartment, talking, restoring their sense of normalcy, putting his struggle with the Turk behind them. "It's all over now," he said. And gradually she came to accept it.

As Penny continued her packing, Darnell pulled from his pocket the slender book he had taken from Tony Arnaud's suitcase. Until now, events had prevented his examining it, but this was his last chance to do it before Bucharest. He would see if the book lived up to its title, *The Orient Express*, in terms of the legends the name alone evoked. Thirty minutes later, he had the answer to that question, and a clue to the events of compartment seven.

"I'll be back soon," he said, and left their compartment. A few steps away, he knocked on the door of compartment seven, still holding the book. Tony Arnaud opened the door. He saw Darnell's expression, glanced down at the book in his hand, and gasped audibly.

Elizabeth, sitting at the window, asked, "What is it, Tony?"

Looking in Darnell's eyes all the time, he called back to her, "I will be gone for a few minutes, *chérie*. Wait here."

He stepped into the hall beside Darnell and ran a hand through his hair. "You have found me out. Now . . . ?"

"Now, we see Manager Bayard, and you make a full breast of your little scheme."

"I am ready." Arnaud sighed. "No more deception."

Bayard sat at the far end of the dining room speaking with the chef. As Darnell and Arnaud approached, he dismissed the chef. "John. M'sieur Arnaud. Is something wrong?"

"Yes," Darnell said. "A little something that Tony wishes to tell you. Correct, Tony?"

Arnaud nodded.

The three sat at the table. Bayard spoke to Darnell. "We have three men guarding the Turk. He'll be secure until we reach Bucharest in an hour . . . Now, M'sieur Arnaud?"

Darnell placed the book on the table between them, and Bayard glanced at it.

"That book," Arnaud said, "caused it all. That, and what the teacher told me."

"The teacher?" Bayard frowned, and glanced at Darnell.

"The one who was in your compartment seven. She lives in the apartment building where I have my studio. She told me all about her trip, how she bought this book, and got her fare refunded . . ."

Bayard finished it, ". . . by pretending to see a phantom. Yes, I understand, now . . . First class is expensive."

Darnell said, "The book has a complete, graphic story about the Duchess Maria and her bridegroom, the slashing, even a drawing of how the Duchess must have looked that night." He paused. "The key passages are underlined." He picked up the book and opened it to a page. "Notice the writing in the margin—'Read this part to Elizabeth.'"

Arnaud ran both hands through his hair. "It was

wrong, and I can't blame the teacher—the idea was mine. When I heard she received full fare, I thought—what if Elizabeth had a nightmare? She always does over anything like that. And she did. Then I had to go on with the deception . . . I'm glad it's over now."

"And what do you propose to do?" Bayard looked at him sternly, but turned aside to Darnell and winked.

"I am not a thief." He pulled papers from his pocket and laid them in front of Bayard. "Here are the refund vouchers you gave us. I will find a way to pay for our passage, I'll sell my paintings, I'll do . . . I'll do whatever I have to."

Bayard rested a hand on the young man's shoulder. "You kept your part of the bargain. You have told no one on the train. I am sure you will tell no one after you leave the train . . . ?"

"I swear it!"

"Then we will say no more of money." He pushed the vouchers back toward Arnaud. "You and your wife take your trip to Greece, come back to Bucharest, and return on the Express to Paris. Call it a gift . . . for your small one." Bayard smiled at Arnaud's surprise. "I have my sources of information."

Tony Arnaud's face broke into a wide grin as he picked up the vouchers. He took Bayard's hand and shook it vigorously, smiling all the time. At last he stopped, and stood. "I must tell Elizabeth." He whirled about to head back toward their room.

Darnell pressed the book into his hand. "A reminder of how you can easily become entangled in dangerous webs of deception."

"Never again!" Tony Arnaud said, and hurried away.

Bayard looked across the table at Darnell. "So—

you have solved this case, John. No apparition, no ghost—just the financial needs of an old woman and the folly of a young man."

"Then you are satisfied."

"Of course, of course." He paused. "And the other things—the murders, the Turk, the Prince." He shuddered. "If you had not been aboard, only *le bon Dieu* knows what could have happened—perhaps the death of a Prince on my line! There is no way to thank you for what you did."

"Certainly a journey to remember. But if we'd known what would happen . . ."

"*Mon ami!* You'd have wanted a larger fee!" Bayard laughed at his own joke, a sense of great relief sounding in his voice.

Across the way, Madame Morgana cleared her throat loudly. "I overheard. Don't be too certain Elizabeth did not experience what she claimed."

Darnell glanced at Bayard then cocked an eye at the psychic. "You could believe she actually saw an apparition?"

"The line between dreams and reality is very vague."

Bayard rose. "I am satisfied. M'sieur Arnaud confessed his scheme was to save money. The matter is settled. Professor?"

Darnell spread his arms. "Your Board should be satisfied—and yet, I will do one more thing to complete this investigation."

"Yes?"

"On our return trip in a few days, we will stay in number seven—keep it open for us, Pierre."

"Of course, but—"

"I think your Board will want to have that last proof that phantoms do not haunt that compartment."

"It is unnecessary—but I will arrange it." Bayard

glanced at his watch. "We near Bucharest, and I must prepare. I will see you when you leave." Bayard walked toward the first-class coach.

Madame Morgana looked at Darnell. "Remember, there are more things on heaven and earth, Professor, than are dreamt of in your philosophy."

Darnell shook his head. "You and Shakespeare may be right in some ways. But the only phantoms this train will have are its memories—the remembrances of an innocent Major Coulton, the dangerous Ovar Pasha, and an unlucky spy, General Eberhardt. Passengers who leave this train will never forget these unfortunates. They will become the real phantoms of the Orient Express—haunting our memories."

Chapter Twenty-Seven

In less than an hour, the Orient Express, its speed cut by engineer Duncan to the slower, three-quarter time of the churning wheels, chugged into the Bucharest station. With a sharp and hissing release of steam, the wheels ground to a halt at the wooden platform. Doors were flung open and passengers began to alight. Pierre Bayard stood just outside the doors to the first-class sleepers to offer parting thanks and good-byes to his guests.

Philippe Cuvier came out to the platform first, and gave a fleeting smile to Anna Held nearby. He formed the word "Good-bye" silently with his lips. Cuvier ceremoniously shook Bayard's outstretched hand and accepted the train Manager's *"Merci beaucoup."* Picking up his suitcase, he walked across the platform without looking back or saying a word.

Darnell stepped out holding Penny's hand. They stood by Bayard's side, chatting with him, waiting for their bags.

Darnell observed the other passengers as they alighted. He, more than anyone else, knew the extent to which the lives of each of them had been affected by the trip.

Anna Held, holding her dog Henri, was quickly

joined by Arturo Donatello—still known as Anton
Donnelli to all but Darnell and her. Donatello shook
hands with Darnell. "Thank you for all your help.
We'll never forget it." He paused and looked about.
"I had no chance to tell you—the man I saw go into
the Major's room that morning, it was the Turk, the
one who was killed, Gaspar."

Darnell gave him a wry smile. "Yes, I know . . . I
hope you keep your commitment to yourself." Darnell knew Penny was looking at him quizzically. He
had a story to tell her.

Donatello and Anna said their good-byes to Bayard, whose voice echoed his repetitive words of
thanks for them, as he had offered to each passenger.
They walked away, arm in arm. A porter followed
them with their bags.

Mata Hari—still Margaret Zelle to all on the train
other than Darnell, Penny, Bayard, and the Madame,
who shared the secret of her name and her past—
stood opposite the Darnells, waiting.

Donald Brand and Agatha Miller came out and
stood apart, and talked. After shaking hands with
her formally, Brand took his cases and stepped across
the wooden slats to Darnell.

"I owe you my life, Professor," he said.

Darnell smiled. "Open your briefcases in the future, Donald. Some surprises can be deadly."

Brand continued to the exit. Near the far end of
the platform he looked back and waved once to Agatha Miller. She raised her hand, then looked away.

Agatha moved to the side of Darnell and Penny
and said the pleasantries of good-bye, but went on,
"I'll never forget this trip, Professor—the mysteries,
the cyanide. I've made lots of notes and have some
good ideas. Some of this will be in my books someday, because one of them will be an Orient Express

mystery. Of course, it'll be imaginary." She laughed. "Unlike you, my detective will be fictional—I still have to invent him."

Although they were going on, the Arnauds stepped out on the platform to talk with Agatha Miller and Penny, and to thank Darnell.

When the Arnauds said their good-byes to Agatha Miller, she told them, "I'm so envious. Constantinople and Greece. I've always wanted to go to such places. Someday . . ."

The two Greeks stepped out and walked over to Bayard's side. Demetrius said, "Just a breath of air, and to stretch."

At that moment, all eyes turned to look at the spectacle of two conductors bringing Heggar Pasha off the train and forward toward Bayard. The Turk's hands were bound behind him, and each conductor held one of the Pasha's arms in a strong grip. They stopped at Bayard's side, as the others on the platform watched.

"I've sent for the local *gendarmes*," Bayard said. "They should be here in moments."

The Turk glared at Bayard, then his gaze fell on Mata Hari, and his lips turned up at the corners.

Her eyes flared wide, and as others watched in awe, a silver blade appeared in her hand seemingly from nowhere and flashed in the sunlight as she rushed forward toward the Turk. The Turk shrank back.

But in that instant, there was another abrupt movement. Demetrius jumped in front of Mata Hari and growled, "No, give it to me!" He wrenched the knife from her hand and in the same sweeping motion thrust it deep into the chest of Heggar Pasha, directly over his heart.

Elizabeth Arnaud screamed, and everyone on the platform looked at the bloody tableau.

The Turk gave a guttural cry, ending in a liquid gurgle as blood escaped his lips. His head rolled back, then forward.

His body slumped, the leather knife hilt with a silver cross bar protruding still from his tunic. The surprised conductors could not hold the now-dead weight of the man's body, which slid from their grasp to the platform. Blood formed a bright red circle on the outer cloth of his coat.

"*Mon Dieu! Mon Dieu!*" Bayard bent down to examine the man, who had collapsed on the wooden slats. The eyes were blank, staring now, and bubbles of blood formed on the Turk's lips.

Agatha Miller stooped down also and touched a pulse point on the Turk's neck. She shook her head, and looked up at Bayard. "He's gone."

"That's the knife that killed the General," Darnell said. "She must have taken it."

Tony Arnaud jumped over and grabbed the arms of the Greek, pinning them behind the man's back. Demetrius did not resist. His face had a calmness inconsistent with his action. The conductors took the Greek from the grasp of Tony Arnaud and held him securely between them.

As a half dozen police ran up, Bayard said, "There is a change in plans." He gestured at the body. "I sent you to take him into custody, but this man killed him. Now you can take them both. I'll come along later and give you a statement."

Mata Hari stood with her hands over her mouth, her eyes filled with tears. "It was for Klaus," she said, sobbing.

"I don't know what they'll do with you," Bayard said to her, softly, "but you'll have to go with them and give a statement. The knife was first in your hands. But I'll talk with them."

Madame Morgana stepped down onto the platform from her compartment. "I saw it all from my window. A final tragedy of this trip," she said. "I had a feeling . . ."

She put an arm around Mata Hari's shoulder. "Your new experiences, your new dangers, are starting. I'll go with you to the police station, as your witness. This time, you escaped your destiny. But next time . . . ?" She shook her head. "You must master your own fate."

The Madame approached Darnell, handing him an envelope. "Before I go, I give this to you and your wife," she said. "Of course, you can look at it later, after all this."

Darnell frowned, stuffing the envelope in his pocket. "I hope you can help this woman. The police have their killer."

The Madame nodded. "I feel it will be all right." She stepped to one side and spoke quietly with Mata Hari.

Bayard ran a hand through his hair. "What a trip!"

"It's over now," Darnell said. "You can relax."

"Not quite. I must see the gendarmes. And the Prince's car is to be moved to a siding. His escorts arrive soon."

Penny said to Darnell, "We should say good-bye to the Prince, and Zizi. They've been awfully good to us." She touched the pendant about her neck.

Darnell nodded.

As if on cue, Prince Carol's court diplomat, Danya Petruso, arrived, breathless, at the train's door, and came out on the platform. "Oh, you are still here. Thank God!" He walked up to Darnell. "The Prince would like very much to see you and your wife before you go."

Darnell looked at Penny. "Shall we go there now?"

"Somebody read my mind."

Darnell took her arm. "Pierre, we'll be back in a bit."

Bayard consulted his watch. "There's time. I'll stay here until you return."

Darnell said, "One moment," and approached Demetrius. He put a hand on the man's shoulder. "You have friends in high places. I'm sure they will take everything the Turk did into account in considering what you did. I'll testify if you need it. We'll be here for a few days."

Demetrius nodded. "Thank you, but it will be all right."

Four of the police were moving down the platform already, carrying the body of the Turk. The other two, standing on either side of Demetrius, clapped handcuffs on him, and led him away after the others. Madame Morgana and Mata Hari followed, accompanied by one officer. Her hands were unshackled.

Darnell and Penny followed Petruso back into the railway car. "Lead on, Danya," Darnell said.

Pierre Bayard stood alone on the platform now, watching all of them leave. He bit a fingernail. "A good bottle of red," Bayard said softly to himself. "I deserve it."

Chapter Twenty-Eight

Danya Petruso walked rapidly through the dining car with short, mincing steps consistent with his height of five feet six. At the open door of the Prince's car, he pushed it open wider, held it for them, bowed, and waved his hand toward the waiting Prince Carol and Zizi Lambrino.

Prince Carol met them halfway across the room and stretched out his arms. "Professor! John, I'm so pleased you hadn't left yet." He shook Darnell's hand and kissed the air an inch above Penny's. "Zizi and I—we want you to come with us to my home, my father's palace. You can spend a few days with us, before you must return to London."

Darnell looked at Penny, whose smile had broadened as the Prince spoke the words. She nodded at her husband.

He said, "We're overwhelmed. But our answer is easy—yes. By all means. We're honored by your invitation."

Zizi said, "Wonderful! Penny—you and I can spend some time together while you're there."

"I'd like that." Penny beamed.

"Then it's settled," Prince Carol said. "Inform the train Manager you'll stay in my car while they shuttle it to a siding. Then my motorcar will be arriving, and we'll go together."

"I'll tell Bayard right away," Darnell said.

"Your wife may stay here with us. Just bring your bags in. Danya will help you with that."

Zizi took Penny's arm and walked with her toward the window seat. As Darnell left the car, he heard Zizi offering Penny champagne.

On the platform, Darnell advised Bayard of the Prince's offer. He noticed their bags had been brought out.

Bayard shook Darnell's hand vigorously. "Then I'll say good-bye, here. What a wonderful experience you will have. The Royal Palace!"

"Remember—we will return on this same train. Keep compartment seven for us." Darnell noted the new schedule for the train's return trip to Paris. "We'll be here to board the Wednesday noon train."

"Then, *au revoir, mon ami!*" Bayard took Darnell in his arms quickly and embraced him. "How can I ever thank you?"

"Just have some champagne chilled on the return trip. We'll drink a last toast together—to the Orient Express phantom!"

Petruso took the heavier bags, Darnell picked up the other cases, and they retraced their steps to the Prince's car. An hour was involved for the transfer of the car to a siding, during which the four talked, enjoyed drinks, and recalled the experiences of the trip. Within an hour after the car was secured, they were ensconced in the magnificence of the Crown Prince's palace.

The first day, Prince Carol took them on a complete tour of the palace. At dinner that night, he introduced them to his father and mother, Crown

Prince Ferdinand and Princess Marie. Later the same night the Prince informed them he had heard news that Demetrius, the Greek, had been spirited away from jail by his confederates, and disappeared.

Prince Carol took Darnell aside and said, "The man did me and the world a service. I'm not displeased his men were able to effect his release." And the Prince winked.

Darnell knew what that meant. The Prince had owed the Greek a debt. Now the debt was paid.

On their last night at the palace, John and Penny Darnell enjoyed a state dinner with the royal family and their special guests. Yet Darnell saw that Prince Carol, without the company of Zizi Lambrino at the table, was far from his usual relaxed, exuberant self. He fidgeted, looked at his watch, and seemed anxious for the dinner to end.

After the dinner that night, Prince Carol, walking with Zizi in the garden, met the Darnells at an appointed place, and confided in them. "Zizi wasn't invited to the dinner because of her lower standing, as a mere secretary. Sometimes my father infuriates me. But this won't happen again. We're to be married," he said. His eyes sparkled as he looked at Zizi. "Of course, at first it will have to be secret, because my father would never approve of it. But they'll grow to accept her."

"That's wonderful," Penny said. The four sat on marble benches and talked for an hour of the marriage plans.

Later, in their room, Penny said, "John, how can they bear this? I couldn't *stand* that secrecy."

He swooped her up in his arms and said, "One of the little advantages of *not* being a Prince! To marry the woman of your choice without a lot of interference."

*   *   *

The following morning, after Darnell and Penny exchanged poignant good-byes with Prince Carol and Zizi, the Prince's private motorcar—a *limousine*, Prince Carol called it—took the Darnells to the station to board the west-bound Orient Express, for Paris.

Bayard was at the door of the first-class coach to greet them, and had arranged a special reunion luncheon for himself and the Darnells. The table was serviced personally by Chef Voisseron, who provided special dishes and his best wines.

While they felt a sense of mystery and déjà vu as they turned out the lights in compartment seven that first night, the sleep of John and Penny Darnell was uninterrupted, as it was the next two nights, until the train pulled into the Gare de Lyon in Paris. Darnell had expected no less, but was pleased Bayard could now present that to his Board as further proof that no apparitions, phantoms, or ghosts existed in compartment seven.

"It is finished," Bayard said as they parted. "Your fee has been deposited in your bank—and my Chairman said to double what we had agreed to—for your, shall we say, special services." He smiled. "And remember, John, under our arrangements, you will have another all-expense-paid trip on the Orient Express waiting for you, whenever you wish. Perhaps a second honeymoon?"

Penny said, "I'll make sure John doesn't forget."

The Darnells' trip back through Paris and across the Channel to England and London proceeded much more quickly than their outbound adventure. By Sunday noon they were home.

As they stepped across the threshold of their flat,

Darnell was pleased to see the broad smiles of Sung, their valet, and his son Ho San greeting them.

"Welcome home, Professor, and Mrs.," Sung said, his face creased with a smile. "We miss you. London misses you. Cases pile up."

Penny looked at Darnell. "It sounds like our honeymoon is over."

Chapter Twenty-Nine

The following morning, Darnell smiled across the breakfast table at Penny. "It's good to be home."

She matched his smile. "Will you stay awhile?"

"As a matter of fact—"

"Oh, no."

"Just a short trip to the Foreign Office. I have something I must deliver to them."

An hour later he sat across from the Foreign Secretary. Two aides sat at either side of the Secretary's massive mahogany desk. Darnell was amused to see the only items on the polished surface were the Secretary's telephone and two pens, set in marble inkwells. The piece of paper he would soon hand the Secretary would spoil the pristine nature of the desktop.

"I regret being mysterious about what I have to give you," Darnell began.

"This office is used to mystery," the Foreign Secretary said.

Darnell went on, "The nature of this message and the source of it were so confidential and indicated such ramifications that I thought your eyes only should see it."

Secretary Beckingham cleared his throat. "Quite, quite. Now, may we . . . ?"

"A little background, first. I'm sure you've heard of the events on the Orient Express."

"Yes. yes. The death of Major Coulton. Young Brand carried on well. The bomb, of course. And a German General and two Turks died?"

"That's true. This document, which appears to be of British origin, was originally in Major Coulton's briefcase, which had been stolen by the General. That case was later taken by Heggar Pasha, the Turk who was killed. I retrieved the case and found this document."

"You recovered a document." He stifled a yawn.

"Yes. And I think it has momentous significance." Darnell handed the Secretary the single sheet of paper he had been carrying since his last confrontation with Heggar Pasha in the Turk's compartment.

Secretary Beckingham cleared his throat again. "We see what you call 'momentous' pronouncements in this room every day, each more compelling than its predecessor. The world, as you know, is teetering on the brink of war, and . . . Well, let's see what this one says." He unfolded the sheet, laying it in front of him on the shiny surface of his desk. He adjusted his spectacles and stared at the words. They had been written using a typewriter.

"There will be an assassination attempt on a young world leader! This will occur in the summer of 1914 in Sarajevo. This attempt must be prevented or it could precipitate a war, the likes of which the world has never known. The authorities in Sarajevo must investigate radical organizations, especially the Black Hand."

"That note," Darnell said, "was in this envelope. As you can see, someone wrote on the envelope in English, 'British Embassy.' "

"Do you know where this came from, who wrote this on the typewriter, and who addressed the envelope?"

Darnell shook his head.

The Secretary's eyes narrowed. He ran a finger inside his collar. "I gather you believe an Englishman wrote this?"

"You judge. The words of the note are in English. The note was in your Major Coulton's case. The envelope was addressed in large, block printing to the British Embassy. And the Germans wanted to steal it."

"Very well, very well. Thank you, Professor Darnell. This office will take it under advisement."

Darnell's forehead creased. "But—you need to take action."

"We will. We will study it carefully, be assured of that."

"It's an assassination, Mr. Secretary!"

"Perhaps, perhaps. We get so many reports . . ." The gray-haired man sighed and removed his glasses.

Darnell stood. "All right. I've done my part. If you need me, you know where to reach me."

In the hallway outside the office, he shook his head and exhaled a deep breath. "Blithering idiot!" he said to himself, in a loud voice. An attendant standing near the door glanced sharply at him. Darnell turned on his heel and strode out of the building.

By the time Darnell returned to their flat, his temper had cooled off and he had resigned himself to accepting the government's promise to study the message. From Beckingham's attitude, however, he suspected they might file it, without any action.

Darnell shook his head. Maybe the Foreign Office knew more about it than he did. Maybe they had their own priorities. All he knew was three men had died because of that scrap of paper.

When he reached the flat, Penny crossed the entryway and threw her arms around him. "Sung has just finished preparing lunch. Let's go in."

"And then?"

"Do you have the afternoon off?"

"The afternoon, the evening, the night."

"Wonderful! No phantoms, and no anxious ladies."

Sung had outdone himself preparing the luncheon dishes, remarking to Penny that the Professor would want "good-old-fashioned English food," as Darnell often called it. Roast beef and Yorkshire pudding, peas, carrots, potatoes.

"It's so nice to be home," Penny said, as they relaxed on the divan in the sitting room. "Spring is coming." She loosened his tie and smoothed his hair back from his forehead. "Upstairs," she added, "there's even a soft breeze blowing."

Darnell nodded. "Yes—but there's something I've saved for a time when everything was behind us. The note Madame Morgana gave me at the station in Bucharest."

"I remember. She was rather mysterious about it."

"Here." He extracted an envelope from his coat pocket. "I haven't opened it yet. She said it concerned both of us, and our Orient Express adventure."

"I wonder what her last message is."

"Open it, and we'll see." He handed the unopened envelope to her.

She slipped a fingernail under the flap to open the

envelope. Inside was a single sheet of paper, which she pulled out. "Shall I read it?"

"Aloud, please." Darnell took a last sip of coffee and looked at Penny expectantly.

"All right. It's her writing."

Darnell thought of Madame Morgana at the Prince's party in the Orient Express dining car, her beads jangling as she gestured, reciting her verses warning of war and death.

Penny's mellow voice broke through his thoughts. "Well, here goes."

> *"The Orient Express spawned a dozen dreams*
> *but what happened wasn't all it seems.*
> *We talked of war, of destiny and fate,*
> *yet in our hearts were thoughts of love, not hate.*
>
> *Young marrieds, in love, brought new life.*
> *A Prince will take his lover for his wife.*
> *A dancer found true love could melt her heart.*
> *An actress sang her songs, and learned her part.*
>
> *The engineer had his own love—the iron beast.*
> *The chef fulfilled his art with one great feast.*
> *The manager's desires were very plain—*
> *he loved his passengers, and his train.*
>
> *And you, Professor, love mysteries of life.*
> *Yet nothing more than Penny, your sweet wife.*
> *This riddle you must strive to understand—*
> *Can love and mystery walk hand in hand?"*

Penny was silent for a moment after reading the verses. She rested her hand on Darnell's shoulder. "It seems the Madame's gloomy predictions did not reveal all of her. She created a cloak of mystery about her, but at heart, she was a romantic."

Darnell said, "So she sends us a message, a challenge—to solve the mystery of love."

Penny teased. "Shall we call in Sherlock Holmes?"

He shook his head. "No. The only thing Holmes loved was solving his mysteries. He admired Irene Adler, but he never really loved a woman. So we'll have to face the Madame's challenge ourselves—and solve that mystery together." He smiled. "Shall we?"

He stood, took her hands, and pulled her up to him. She hooked her arm in his, and they walked together toward the staircase. John Darnell felt the tingle of Penny's hair touch his cheek as a soft breeze carrying a hint of spring blew across the room. He took a deep breath. This case was closed.

Epilogue

Two months later, on June 28, 1914, at their dinner table, John and Penny Darnell heard the insistent voices of newsboys on the street hawking their newspapers, shouting news of the assassination in Sarajevo of Archduke Francis Ferdinand of Austria-Hungary and his wife by a member of a radical society.

"War is sure to come now," Darnell said. He thumped the table with his fist. "But if I'd only pushed that damned Foreign Secretary harder, many deaths could have been prevented."

Penny touched his hand. "Don't be hard on yourself, John. How could you know the Foreign Office wouldn't investigate? You're not psychic."

Darnell nodded. "I can't forget Madame Morgana's quatrains, her images of strawberry fields red with blood and those nameless legions of the dead she saw marching into history. She wrote of a fallen world leader. Now we know who she meant."

The passengers of the fateful Orient Express trip of April 1914 traveled twisted and tangled paths in the months and years that followed that trip, both during and after the war . . .

A few years later, Elizabeth Hopkins Arnaud told her little daughter how they bought her a Gypsy shawl when she was still unborn, at the train stop in Budapest. Elizabeth never forgot the image of the bloody apparition of the Duchess she was convinced she saw in compartment seven of the legendary train, and would occasionally dream of her. When her daughter became old enough, she told her of the woman she believed she'd seen on the train.

The life of the Duchess Maria, whose near-death experience as a young woman became legend, and Sir Basil Zaharoff, who saved her, culminated after many years of romantic liaisons when Maria and Sir Basil were married in 1926.

Madame Morgana, for her part, felt the accounts of the apparition were as real as any she had ever experienced. She told the story many times over in more and more exaggerated form in quatrains that brought chills to her clients and audiences.

Mata Hari returned to France after war broke out, but not with a desire to dance on the stage. She became the most notorious female spy of the twentieth century.

During the war, she was convicted of spying for Germany and causing the deaths of many Frenchmen. She was held in prison and, in anguish, endured a long ordeal of lonely imprisonment and questioning there. Finally, Mata Hari was executed in 1917 by a French firing squad.

Prince Carol secretly married the great love of his young life, Zizi Lambrino, during World War I. Painfully, their marriage was annulled as not suitable for the royal family. Years later, Prince Carol succeeded to his father's throne as supreme monarch of Rumania. Zizi was not at his side.

Anna Held returned to New York City, and in 1916

resumed her career as a singer and dancer, starring in lavish musical stage extravaganzas. She did not remarry. In 1918, she died of myeloma, a rare form of cancer some said was caused by lacing up her corset too tightly in order to achieve her famed hourglass figure.

Arturo Donatello remained true to his promise and gave up his lucrative but dangerous career as a jewel thief in exchange for a quiet life as a hotel manager in Rome. At night on his balcony, he often thought of Anna Held. When news of her death reached him, the full realization of his loss could only be drowned in the uncounted bottles of wine he consumed that week.

Caught in a second attempt to sell his company's aircraft secrets, Bryan Stark was dismissed by Geoffrey de Havilland and left the field of aviation research.

Philippe Cuvier, who built a reputation as an aggressive player in the world of finance, was shot by an irate purchaser of securities who discovered they were fraudulent and worthless.

Donald Brand returned to England and continued his diplomatic career until 1916, when he joined the British army. Within two months, after brief training and hurried embarkation to France, he was riddled by machine-gun bullets in his first battle on a blood-soaked field near the forests of France. Yet he was only one of millions who were sacrificed or gave themselves for causes they only barely understood.

Agatha Miller married her fiancé, Archibald Christie, on Christmas Day, 1914. As Agatha Christie, a name which became world famous, she wrote mystery stories, plays, and novels, her first novel published six years later. A few years after the publication of that novel, and at the time of an impending breakup of her marriage with Christie, she disappeared for ten days in a real-life mystery, explained as due to amnesia.

After her divorce, she later married an archaeologist, and was able to do the two things she loved best—travel and write. In the early 1930s, Agatha Christie penned her novel *Murder on the Orient Express,* in which her fictional Belgian detective, Hercule Poirot, solved a bizarre murder on the exotic train.

In the years that followed, an era in which both common folk and prominent citizens alike reported ghostly sightings, based on superstitions and fears of the occult, Professor John Darnell solved many other such mysteries in which he and Penny were enmeshed by choice and by chance.

But he and Penny always regarded this case as one of the most sensational. And, because of their shared experiences with the people aboard the train, and their special memories of each of them, they would never forget the excitement and danger of this adventure—on the Orient Express.

John and Penny Darnell return in . . .
The Case of the 2nd Seance
by Sam McCarver

Join John and Penny in another adventure
with mysteries to solve and murder afoot
—in London's dark, sinister world
of psychics and seances!

Coming soon from Signet